Cock-A-Doodle-Doo

ESSENTIAL TRANSLATIONS SERIES 54

Guernica Editions Inc. acknowledges the support of
the Canada Council for the Arts and the Ontario Arts Council.
The Ontario Arts Council is an agency of the Government of Ontario.
We acknowledge the financial support of the Government of Canada through
the National Translation Program for Book Publishing, an initiative
of the *Roadmap for Canada's Official Languages 2013-2018:
Education, Immigration, Communities*, for our translation activities.
We acknowledge the financial support of the Government of Canada.
Nous reconnaissons l'appui financier du gouvernement du Canada.

Cock-A-Doodle-Doo

PAN BOUYOUCAS

Translated by
Maureen Labonté

**GUERNICA
EDITIONS**

TORONTO · CHICAGO
BUFFALO · LANCASTER (U.K.)
2022

Guernica Founder: Antonio D'Alfonso

Michael Mirolla, editor
Cover and interior design: Rafael Chimicatti
Guernica Editions Inc.
287 Templemead Drive, Hamilton (ON), Canada L8W 2W4
2250 Military Road, Tonawanda, N.Y. 14150-6000 U.S.A.
www.guernicaeditions.com

Distributors:
Independent Publishers Group (IPG)
600 North Pulaski Road, Chicago IL 60624
University of Toronto Press Distribution (UTP)
5201 Dufferin Street, Toronto (ON), Canada M3H 5T8
Gazelle Book Services, White Cross Mills
High Town, Lancaster LA1 4XS U.K.

First edition.
Printed in Canada.

Legal Deposit—First Quarter
Library of Congress Catalog Card Number: 2021947265
Library and Archives Canada Cataloguing in Publication
Title: Cock-a-doodle-doo / Pan Bouyoucas ; translated by Maureen Labonté.
Other titles: Cocorico. English
Names: Bouyoucas, Pan, author. | Labonté, Maureen, 1949- translator.
Series: Essential translations series ; 54.
Description: Series statement: Essential translations series ; 54
Translation of: Cocorico.
Identifiers: Canadiana (print) 20210321636 | Canadiana (ebook) 20210321687
| ISBN 9781771837040 (softcover) | ISBN 9781771837057 (EPUB)
Classification: LCC PS8553.O89 C6213 2022 | DDC C843/.54—dc23

-1-

LIKE MANY CANADIAN WRITERS of his generation, Leo Basilius launched his literary career with the publication of a book of poetry. He followed that up, two years later, with a collection of short stories and, four years after that, with a detective novel which catapulted him to the top of the bestsellers' list two weeks after it was released.

This was in 1980. Leo Basilius was thirty years old. In the thirty years that followed, he published 15 other novels in the detective series. Translated into thirty languages, they were praised by critics for their realism, their lean, sober style and their clever, page-turning plotlines which, free of artifice, moved inexorably forward in short, sharp scenes that followed hard one on the other.

The protagonist of Basilius' series was Inspector Vass Levonian, a member of the homicide squad of a large, but fictional, Canadian city. Methodical and headstrong, he was always the best man to solve a case. He never lost his cool or his sense of irony, unless the victim was a child.

"All of us carry the guilt for every aggression committed against a child," he says in *Lost Lights*, Basilius' sixteenth best-seller and the last novel in the series.

Levonian was investigating a series of kidnappings of little girls all under the age of ten. He was so shaken by these crimes that he forgot to take even the most basic precautions and was seriously wounded in his final confrontation with the sadistic pedophile he'd been pursuing for the last three hundred pages.

Shot twice, one of the bullets perforated a carotid and put him into a deep coma. The doctors gave him four chances out of 10 of surviving. Maybe five out of 10 for a fighter like him. But because his brain hadn't received the blood and oxygen it needed for a few minutes, they couldn't predict whether there would be any permanent damage if and when he woke or any conscious mental life left to even speak of.

Seventy percent of Basilius' readers were, god bless them, women and this tragedy unleashed a wave of sympathy for Levonian's plight. They were waiting impatiently for the next novel, eager to find out if their beloved inspector would regain consciousness and what the mental, physical and psychological consequences would be when he did.

The reviewers couldn't care less about the damage the bullets had done. Heroes as profit-making as Levonian don't die, said the most cynical of them. What they wanted to know was why Basilius had opted for such a melodramatic resolution. He didn't need this kind of cliff-hanger ending to sell his next novel.

For the first time in his career, the undisputed master of the Canadian detective novel, so admired for his flair, for the strength and soberness of his work which had earned him national and international prizes in the crime novel genre, refused all requests for interviews, announcing, through his agent, that he had gone off to write his next book. What he didn't say, not even to his agent, was that, at the peak of his writing career, he had decided to drop Inspector Vass Levonian and the detective novel.

Leo Basilius had also fathered a daughter and two sons, all adults today, and had been living with their mother for the past thirty-five years. Her name was Muriel Dubois. She was the only person in whom he confided his desire to give up writing crime fiction.

He said: "I'm sixty years old. My mother died of cancer when she was sixty-three and my father got Alzheimer's at sixty-seven. If those two diseases are hereditary, then, now's the time for me to write about the things I didn't get to write about in my detective novels."

Basilius didn't specify what these things were and Muriel didn't pursue the matter. She knew her husband never discussed his books during their gestation period and did so only rarely when he was in the process of actually writing them. However, she did ask for an explanation when Basilius, who had never altered his work habits in the thirty-five years they had lived together, announced, three months later, that he wanted to go and write on Nysa, the Greek island, where he had written his book of poetry, and asked her to go with him.

"I can't seem to get into my new project," he said. "I need to get away from everything that reminds me of my detective novels."

Basilius had often spoken to his wife about the year he'd spent on Nysa when he was a young man. Muriel was more than happy to visit the island but only for a few days.

"I couldn't spend two years living in a small port at the other end of the Mediterranean. I don't even speak the language. I'd be bored to death."

"I don't speak Greek, either."

"When you write, you turn inward and live with your characters. I think you should go alone. You did it before."

He was twenty-two and everything was new. With age — he realized this during his promotional tours — it had become harder for him to strike up conversations and make small talk with strangers. The people, the cities, the scenery, all seemed the same to him. The same and boring. In fact, he felt that all he did now during these tours was count the days and the hours until he got home again. And besides, he wouldn't be spending all his time writing while he was on Nysa. There were certain pleasures, like meals, he preferred to share with Muriel who, after thirty-five years of marriage, had learned not to force him to talk when he had nothing to say.

By nature, and because she'd travelled much less than he had, Muriel was also better at striking up a conversation with strangers. So, to encourage her, Basilius pointed out that there were lots of ex-pats living on Nysa and most of them spoke either English or French.

Muriel gave in. She agreed to go but for only six months. Even if she did make friends on Nysa, she said, she couldn't spend more than six months without seeing her children and grandchildren.

Basilius knew he couldn't write his new novel in six months. Still, he agreed to her terms. He had to put distance between himself and the body of work he'd devoted thirty years of his life to. He had to cultivate new ground in which to seed his next novel. If he needed more than six months, he'd bring his children and grandchildren over for a visit and, then, he and Muriel could stay on the island for another six months.

The next day, he contacted a rental agency. He told them he wanted a furnished house in the small port town of Nysa where he'd lived when he was twenty-two years old. He specified that the house had to have a view of the sea and Internet access, as well as two bedrooms, one of which had to be air-conditioned. Muriel couldn't stand the heat. He, on the other hand, hated air conditioning and always slept with the windows and shutters open. Basilius also asked that the house not have a third bedroom. When his children visited, he would put them up at a hotel. He needed silence to work and, since his time on the island was limited, he refused to give up even a single minute of the six hours each day he would spend working on his new project.

–3–

THE HOUSE ON NYSA was everything Basilius had hoped it would be. He was so pleased that, as soon as he and Muriel had visited it, he took her on a tour of the little port town where he'd started writing at twenty-two. He particularly wanted to show her the jugs of fresh water which he wrote about in his collection of short stories inspired by the island.

It's a sacred custom on this arid island where you can count the number of fresh water springs on the fingers of one hand, he'd written. *You can refuse anyone anything here except a glass of water. And to ensure that a thirsty passer-by doesn't have to knock and beg, a jug of fresh water is placed in a recess in the wall to the left or the right of every door.*

Muriel found this charming but, after travelling by plane and boat for twenty-two hours, all she wanted to do was unpack, slip into her nightgown and go to sleep.

Basilius, on the other hand, was so excited he spent the rest of the evening rearranging the furniture in the room that was going to be his office. He set up his laptop and laid out pens, notepads and dictionaries on his worktable eager to get started on this new phase of his life.

By the time everything was where he wanted it, the entire island was asleep. Still, Basilius had to walk down to the shore before going to bed. He wanted to touch the sea. Feel it. It had served him so well the first time he'd come to Greece for a year after university like so many young people did at the time. Many of them were aspiring artists. Some had become famous. He had. Not with the book of poems he wrote on Nysa. Nor with the collection of short stories he'd written when he got back to Canada recounting his time on the island. Between the publication of the two, he'd met Muriel and had his first child. In order to provide for his young family, he'd taken a job as the editor of the Policemen's Union monthly newsletter. The job lasted four years and it inspired his first detective novel, *Janus & Associates*, which sold more than a hundred thousand copies and was translated into ten languages.

Fifteen crime novels and as many million copies later, Basilius was again standing on the shores of the island where he'd written his book of poems.

The night was soft and full. The smell of jasmine floated on the air, and the sea, bathed in moonlight, stretched out calmly all the way to Asia.

Basilius bent down and filled his hand with water, raised it to his lips and said to the sea: "I need one word to get me dreaming again. Help me find that word."

No sooner had he spoken than he felt a presence behind him.

He turned expecting to see his wife. Muriel would sometimes wake at night and have trouble getting back to sleep. But instead of her, Basilius saw Inspector Vass Levonian standing there looking like Russell Crane, the American actor who'd played him in the movie adaptations of three of his novels.

Levonian didn't look remotely the same as he had at the end of the last novel — comatose and surrounded by life-support equipment with tubes feeding him and breathing for him. Quite the opposite. The police officer was as healthy and as grumpy as usual.

"I've never seen the sea," he said to his creator. "Never seen the horizon either. Just bricks and cement."

Basilius ignored this reproach, turned his back on his character and headed up to the house.

-4-

BASILIUS SPENT THE FIRST few days taking Muriel around to all the places he had been to when he was young and everything he saw filled his heart with joy and inspired him to write poetry.

They started in the town of Nysa and its small port.

Neither had changed much except for a tiny detail here and there. There were still water jugs in an alcove to the side of many of the doors but the jugs were now empty. You could buy bottled water everywhere. Peddlers who had once hawked their wares at the top of their lungs had traded their donkeys for pickup trucks equipped with megaphones. The number of road-side shrines built to honour the memory of the victims of car accidents had increased with the proliferation of cars and motorcycles. On the other hand, the number of buildings along the waterfront hadn't. Space was at a premium and, by law, it was forbidden to demolish old heritage buildings. That said, most of them, like the house where Basilius had lived for a year, had been renovated and their ground floors converted into a bar, a minimart or a tourist shop. And the islanders, the older ones, like his landlady, had moved on to the graveyard and the younger ones had aged by at least four decades. Basilius didn't recognize a soul.

After wandering through the town's maze of narrow streets and alleyways for two hours, Basilius and Muriel made their way back to the port, bought some groceries and then settled at a table on the terrace of a café and ordered something to drink.

Back in the day, this place had only served Greek coffee. Hippies wandered the earth and there was always someone there discussing the state of the world and the problems facing humanity and how they proposed to change it all. Some stayed for only a month. Others, like Basilius, left after a year. Loraine, a young American woman Basilius had had a brief love affair with, had decided to go to Athens and teach English. Was she still there? Did she remember the small creek where they used to swim in the nude?

When you're travelling, you're much more conscious of the fact that everything comes to an end. He had written this in a short story inspired by Loraine entitled "The Creek". *That's why every moment is so special, so enchanting. In real life, it can take weeks to become intimate with someone. When you're travelling, a three-minute conversation is enough. And the connections with people that fate places on your path can be all that much more intense for being so brief.*

Today, the foreigners sitting in the café all had cameras in their hands and, between sips of *cappuccino* or *latte*, they took pictures of each other with a fisherman repairing his nets in the background. In other words, they were tourists stopping on the island for a day or two.

When it came to antique ruins, Nysa only had one Byzantine monastery perched on the top of the highest hill overlooking the town and, on the west coast, on a cliff that dropped steeply into the sea, there were the remains of a temple dedicated to Dionysos — three stone blocks of what was once the floor and two pieces of a column. The island hippies used to gather there to watch the sun set.

Basilius took his wife to see the monastery and the ruins on the second day after their arrival.

On the third day, they walked over hills spotted here and there with chapels and the ruins of wind mills. After following a long shoreline broken by creeks and bays, they ended up in a small village where everyone was Greek. The foreigners they met as they walked all carried cameras and Basilius started to worry that they wouldn't find anyone Muriel could become friends with. Then, on the fourth day, in the pharmacy where they'd stopped to buy sun screen, they struck up a conversation with an Australian painter in his 50's by the name of Farley Marsh. He'd been living on the island for five years.

"A lot of strangers live on Nysa," he told them. "But, like my partner and myself, they prefer to live in more remote areas surrounded by trees that hide their houses from the road and from the tourists."

The painter knew Basilius by reputation. When he heard that he and his wife planned on spending six months on the island, he invited them to a méchoui he was having with friends at his house that evening. Basilius didn't eat meat but accepted the invitation in the hope that Muriel would perhaps meet people she could make friends with and talk to while he was locked away in his office writing.

-5-

DURING HIS FIRST STAY ON NYSA, the foreigners living on the island were mostly young people who wanted to live on the fringes of society. But now Greece was part of the European Union and only the grey-haired, middle class with money like him could afford to stay on the island for any length of time, especially, if they wanted to live in a house overlooking the Aegean.

That was the first thing Basilius realized when he arrived at the méchoui dinner being given by the painter and his companion, an astrologist, now retired, by the name of Sean Costello. The painter was still painting.

"Since I arrived here, I've been painting chairs mostly," he said to Basilius and Muriel as he showed them his work which was leaning against the walls of the house. "There are chairs everywhere on this island. On every balcony and veranda. In front of every shop and every house. Chairs of every colour, shape and size, made of every material imaginable. They seem to say to the passer-by: Come over here, sit down and tell me all about yourself. You see, it's thanks to this curiosity and this interactivity that, in Ancient Greece, on these very shores, the islanders succeeded in transforming the beliefs and superstitions that travellers brought back from the Orient into free thought, succeeded in building a theory of evolution twenty-five centuries before Darwin, and in synthesizing the pyramids and other oriental monuments to the cult of death into simple gravestones engraved with only one word, *Haire* — Be Happy — a word of farewell and of advice — nothing is as good as this good earth and its light. That's what my chairs represent: that curiosity and interaction which, in my humble opinion, are an antidote to the threat of fanaticism and of intolerance on the rise again today and which will inevitably plunge a large portion of humanity back into darkness."

The simple, straightforward way Farley Marsh had spoken to them earlier at the pharmacy had disappeared. Basilius understood why when Marsh introduced him to the other guests as the "king of crime fiction" whose main character, Inspector Levonian, had sent Basilius and his detective novels to the top of bestseller lists all over the world. Like the painter and his chairs with their hackneyed, dime-store symbolism, as soon as the others found out that Basilius was a novelist, they started speaking in long, complex sentences, trying to put their charm, sophistication and erudition on display, furnishing all sorts of details about their lives, using carefully chosen words, convinced that, one day, they might find themselves, under a pseudonym of course, in the next novel by the "King of Crime," the one he had surely come to the island to write.

But Basilius had come to the island to get away from everything that reminded him of his detective novels, so it was particularly difficult for him to be brought back to it during dinner. The guests wanted to know why a man who was so gentle and charming and a vegetarian to boot, why would he want to create a world that was so dark and violent. How did he slip into the skin of serial killers and other monsters, day after day after day?

Basilius tried to lead the conversation onto more neutral ground. Food. He pointed out that he wasn't really a vegetarian. Perhaps he didn't eat meat but he very much enjoyed fish. However, the others weren't to be distracted and they insisted on finding out how he came up with the storylines, the machinations and the violence that made up his hero's day-to-day life. And his poor wife. Did she sleep well at night lying next to a man who, day after day, descended into a hell made of death and murder?

He was used to these kinds of questions. He was asked them in interviews and at every book fair, public reading and writers' conference he attended. He had answers at the ready and he doled out some of them to give Muriel time to make friends. Because some of the guests had read at least one of his books, he felt obliged to answer out of common courtesy. His answers proved to be so satisfying that the guests started wishing there would be a murder on Nysa so that they might see the king of crime at work, as though Basilius possessed the same investigative skills as his celebrated detective, Inspector Levonian. A few of them even went so far as to speculate as to whether murder was an act they might actually commit themselves. This led them to the conclusion that, one day, if the Nysian murder was adapted for the screen, Russell Crane and a bevy of stars would come to the island to actually play the parts of the people sitting around the table that evening. Basilius encouraged them along these lines. The last thing he wanted was for them to start comparing his books to detective novels by other writers and then ask him what he thought of his competition.

He talked about Russell Crane whom he had met twice. And the more he talked about the star and the making of the movies based on his novels, the more his dinner companions delighted in the possibility that they might meet Crane someday soon.

–6–

THEY WERE STILL TALKING about movies when a young couple arrived. Alicia and Drew apologized for being late. They'd found an isolated little creek where Alicia had wanted to swim in the nude. After their swim, they fell asleep on the pebble beach and had woken after night fall.

Alicia was Sean Costello's niece. She'd just arrived with her boyfriend to spend the summer at her uncle's house. She had read four of Basilius' novels. Her boyfriend hadn't read even one but he made a point of telling everyone he was a more avid reader than his companion.

"Don't take it personally," he told the King of Crime. "I don't like crime fiction. The characters are all stereotypes and the stories too predictable. But what I find the most off-putting is the pretence that they're exploring the depths, or the underbelly, of the human soul when all they really do is exploit its more perverse and violent sides with a few sociopolitical notions thrown in to ease their conscience."

Basilius was also used to this kind of know-it-all who, in every group, held forth because they liked to debate or show off. He always refused to engage in these kinds of discussions about his novels and decided to let Drew's comments pass. But Alicia sprang to his defense. She asked her boyfriend what he based his brilliant conclusions on if he hadn't read a single one of Leo Basilius' novels.

"All detective novels follow the same formula," he replied "There's a crime which the main character will solve as sure as page twelve follows page eleven."

"Oedipus and Hamlet do the same thing."

"You're putting *Oedipus* and *Hamlet* on the same footing as a crime novel?" he countered indignantly. "Not even Mr. Basilius would do that. He wouldn't dare. Am I right, sir?"

"You're being ridiculous!" Alicia exclaimed. "You can't ask Mr. Basilius to be both judge and accused!"

"Fine. Let time be the judge. Crime writers who were at the top of their form twenty years ago are completely forgotten today. But we still read *Hamlet* and *Oedipus*. Why? Because literature doesn't concern itself with stories which, under the guise of portraying society as it struggles with its demons, pile on killing after killing and other atrocities of the same ilk, without suggesting anything in return other than the old worn-out adage that in the end justice will triumph. Literature, my love, great literature is myth and poetry. It ennobles man and reconciles us with our faults and our virtues."

"If a lot of writers have been forgotten," his love replied with an edge to her voice, "it's because men like you ignored them or burnt their books because they disapproved of the content. Now, if you don't mind, could we talk about something else? These poor people didn't come here tonight to listen to your literary rants. Frankly, your superior attitude is getting on everybody's nerves."

Then, turning to Basilius: "Please forgive him. He just got his doctorate in Comparative Literature." Turning to Muriel, she added: "Mrs. Basilius, tell me, what do you do?"

Finally, someone was showing an interest in Muriel. When she answered that she'd been a nurse but in the last few years, since retiring, she did volunteer work, Alicia said her mother, Sean's sister, who died when she was still a child, had also been a nurse. Alicia stuck to her for the rest of the evening.

"I feel as though I've been adopted by an orphan," Muriel said to her husband when they got home. Then, on a more serious note, she asked him why he hadn't responded to Drew's attack and put the snot, doctorate and all, in his place.

"The crime novel was just an excuse for a lovers' quarrel," Basilius answered. "Those two didn't get there late because they fell asleep after skinny dipping and making love. Something else happened at the creek for her to attack her lover with such virulence and defend a total stranger."

"Still, you might've said something in defense of your work. Unless you agree with him! Is that why you've given up writing detective fiction?"

"I've given up detective novels so I can write about the things that fill me with joy. You, for example. My children, my grand-children."

Moved, his wife slipped her arm through his.

"You were right not to say anything. That know-it-all would've interpreted it as an act of contrition and demolished everything Alicia said in your defense."

Muriel went to bed as soon as they got home. Basilius sat on the terrace because he wanted to look at the sea and clear his mind before sleeping. But no sooner had he sat down, than Levonian appeared and said:

"You have no right to bury me. You hear me? I don't want to die."

WHEN HE CREATED Inspector Vass Levonian, Basilius hadn't planned on a career writing crime fiction. He had decided to use the device of a police investigation to denounce the hypocrisy and racism of certain crown prosecutors, cops, and politicians in the country following a scandal involving a young Native boy who had spent seventeen years in prison for a crime he didn't commit. *Janus & Associates* was steeped in a social reality that was so precise, its denunciation of certain injustices so implacable that for a while the book's protagonist became the emblem of a protest movement that actually succeeded in bringing about a number of changes.

Basilius was flattered and easily persuaded by his agent into making Levonian the hero of his next novel. *Night Calls* was on the bestseller list for forty-two weeks and won the highest distinctions in the crime fiction genre in the United States. Like Drew, the Canadian literary community considered crime fiction to be a sub-genre. Since then, and because of Basilius' success and the proliferation of the genre in movies and on television, there are very few Canadian writers who don't dream of writing a detective novel and selling the movie rights to Hollywood.

Basilius was proud of the novels that followed *Janus &
Associates* and *Night Calls* and he considered a few of them
— and not necessarily the ones which had been praised the
most by the critics and won prizes and awards — amongst
some of the best examples of contemporary crime fiction.
But these novels, along with all the other crime novels now
on the market, the TV police series and films, gave the impression that vice ruled the streets of North America, that
drugs and crime were rampant in every city, and murders
were as frequent as shoplifting in most neighbourhoods.

This was one of the reasons why Basilius had decided to
give up writing detective fiction.

From now on, he wanted to write about the beauty of the
world and its light. He wanted to show that human beings
didn't just have vile impulses. That the impulse to create was
stronger than the one to hate, kill, rape, destroy and steal.

The most difficult task still lay ahead: how to express
this without sounding sentimental or preachy and especially, without repeating himself. Something he was more
and more convinced he'd been doing in his crime fiction.

While he was writing his last crime novel, he started
putting a few ideas on paper. But, when he re-read them, he
realized they sounded like the kind of ideas you get in the
middle of the night and which seem brilliant at the time but
are dull and worthless when you wake up the next morning.

He knew from experience that only a really strong idea
could drive his writing. He also knew that weeks could go
by before that kind of idea came to him. But no matter how
hard he tried, after years of writing detective novels, only
crime stories and murders came to mind. Nothing else.

Even when he went out for some fresh air and to get his mind off things, every street he walked along reminded him of a street in his fictional city, every neighbourhood of a place where a crime he had imagined had taken place. If he saw someone running, it was impossible for him to imagine that the person was trying to catch a bus. Even in places he had never used in his novels, like libraries and museums, if he noticed a man with a closed look, he'd try to guess what could be troubling him and what crime he might be plotting. He'd even imagine the man with his throat slit, and would ask himself why he'd been murdered.

It had become a habit with him as it had for his inspector. Even when he wasn't on duty, Levonian would look at people on the street or in a restaurant and, because of his experience and cop's instincts, his gaze would always linger on someone who looked worried or afraid or someone haunted by a crime in the making or one already committed.

Basilius had to get away from all of it. Away from the dark, violent world he'd created line by line, as well as from the style and conventions of the crime novel. He had a country house where he and Muriel spent the occasional weekend during the year and two months every summer. But he'd even used the cottage as the scene of a crime and a particularly sordid one at that.

"Go back to Nysa," he said to himself one evening as he watched a TV news report on the restoration of the Acropolis. "Go back to Nysa and revisit the places you loved so much before you entered the dark world of crime fiction."

He did. He went back to Nysa.

But the man he wanted to get away from the most had followed him. And now said:

"You don't have the right to bury me. You hear me? I don't want to die."

"Be patient," Basilius said to himself. "He'll go away as soon as you dive into your new project."

-8-

H E GOT UP EVERY MORNING at the first cock's crow. So as not to wake Muriel — she needed a minimum of ten hours sleep — he didn't shower right away like he did back home. Without a noise, he'd splash his face with water, then make himself a cup of coffee which he'd sip slowly on the terrace as he watched the sun come up and give the earth back its colours.

He had always based his stories on real life incidents. The only time he had used a theme as a departure point, the story had seemed forced to him, the plot points glaringly obvious. But all he had for this new project was the theme: the beauty of the world and its light and the fact that man doesn't just have vile instincts, etc. If he was going to succeed in transforming this theme into fiction, he knew he had to find a more concrete starting point, a story with strong characters, emotions and situations, as well as a dramatic motor other than a crime.

It's difficult to concentrate and focus the mind when you're looking at the sea, he'd written some thirty years earlier in his collection of short stories. He was still of that opinion. But rather than locking himself in his office, every morning he would settle down in front of the azure immensity of the Aegean convinced that the wanderings of his spirit inspired by the sea would help him pursue and capture what he was looking for. Sometimes, a word or an image was all it took to trigger the creative process and when this happened, everything fell into place in his head; lines which up until then had seemed to be running parallel suddenly came together. Little by little, the rest followed. Even his main character, Levonian, had been inspired by the voice of a detective he'd interviewed on the telephone for an article he was writing for the police union newsletter. As soon as he heard it, a silhouette appeared, a face and a name. The name was very important. When he found it, his character started to exist on his own.

"Why are you thinking of Levonian right now?" he told himself. "Look at the sea and let your imagination wander, let your mind empty itself of everything Levonian represented."

So, that's what he did, morning after morning, as he sipped his coffee. Every now and then, a word or an idea spawned a flood of images and possibilities and the impasse was transformed into a solid direction to head in and he would write, erase, think, scribble a line or two but everything would scatter and vanish when he realized that, yet again, he was thinking like a writer of detective fiction.

He didn't despair. Slumps were part of the job. And, he'd just arrived on Nysa. Once he got used to his new surroundings and was able to forget them, something would spark probably at a moment when he wasn't thinking about it. And so, he let his spirit and his eyes wander along the shoreline, where he spotted Alicia jogging by. She waved to him. Then, his gaze drifted up and out and got lost over the sea.

He would only leave the terrace when he heard Muriel getting up. Then, he'd lock himself in his office so he could lose himself in his thoughts without feeling observed. He'd emerge when his wife would let him know, from the other side of his office door, that she was going out to do some shopping or to have coffee with one of the people she'd met at the painter's house.

His doubts only returned when he was lying in bed, in the dark. Had his ability to marvel at the world vanished completely over the years? Would he ever succeed in leaving the well-trodden paths of the detective novel and be able to try another approach, another way of writing? He had produced so many well-crafted tales with intricate plot lines and expertly placed twists and surprises that he found all the ideas he'd had during the day boring, naïve, simplistic. Even though he knew that the storylines of many of the great novels he admired could, at first glance, also seem naïve and simplistic and that only beginners dabbled in the complicated and the profound believing that this gave substance and breadth to their stories.

Fed up with tossing and turning, he'd get out of bed. Muriel was a light sleeper. She got up at least five times a night to go to the bathroom. If she saw him moping on the terrace, he knew she would lead him back to her bed and try to take his mind off things like she used to do back home. Basilius didn't feel like getting his mind taken off things so he'd stand at the window of his room for long stretches of time breathing in the sweet smells of the night, or watching an airplane fly over the island the lights on the tips of its wings flashing, or the wild dance of moths and night butterflies clustered around a street lamp below.

On the sixth night, Inspector Levonian, still looking like Russell Crane, appeared in the circle of light cast by the street lamp and looked up at him with a sardonic smile.

On the seventh, Basilius decided to go for a swim before bed and to swim until he was exhausted. That way he'd be certain to fall asleep right away when his head hit the pillow. But, as soon as he left the house, he heard footsteps behind him.

He turned certain he'd see Muriel come to lure him back to her bed.

But there was no one behind him.

He continued down towards the water.

Once again, he heard footsteps.

And, yet again, the footsteps stopped when he did.

The third time, he shouted:

"Levonian! Leave me alone!"

But when he kicked off his sandals, he realised that the sound he'd heard was the sound of his own footsteps echoing on the pebbles of the beach behind him.

–9–

THIS IS HOW BASILIUS spent his second week on Nysa
— he set aside the mornings for his writing project,
had lunch, a nap and then swam in the late afternoon when
the sun wasn't as burning hot and the beach not as busy.

In the evening, he ate dinner with his wife at one of the
seaside cafés.

Muriel, who could turn a trip to the supermarket into an
epic tale, would tell him about her day.

Basilius would listen.

And not just to his wife. He would also listen to what
was being said at the other tables, careful to pick up a word,
a gesture or an anecdote that could be of some use to him.

*Nysa was full of colourful types, real characters, and not just
amongst the strangers, hippies for the most part, wanderers,
looking for nirvana,* he had written in one of the stories inspired by his stay on the island.

*The islanders had lived through two wars — a world war
and a civil war — and would willingly talk about what they
had endured. Sometimes, they even laughed about it as only those
who have cried a lot know how to laugh. Small islands also have
very fertile imaginations. Not much happens in times of peace
and so the islanders attribute a great deal of importance to the
smallest incident. Finally, there were the sailors. Nysa is rocky*

and arid. The island had prospered for a century or two thanks to ship building and trade in natural sponges. The beautiful old houses along the coast attested to this past prosperity. But the production of synthetic sponges and steam ships speeded up the island's decline. Without these two industries and no arable land, the men were forced to spend the greater part of their adult lives on tankers and cargo ships. They returned from these voyages full of tall tales which, with the few words of English they knew, could keep me enthralled for evenings on end.

"Not anymore. Not today," he thought now.

Need and curiosity which had once upon a time pushed the islanders to take to the sea had now been replaced by tourism and money from the European Union. While cheaper manpower from Asia operated the Greek fleets, the descendants of the navigators and sailors who had colonized a good part of the Mediterranean and started the first cosmopolitan civilization of the western world, were sitting around getting fat in their boutiques, bars and cafés. Television was all they needed to satisfy both their curiosity and the call of the open sea. Even though their mastery of English had greatly improved, what they had to say wasn't all that different from the inhabitants of any western city talked about and, more often than not, was addressed to their cellphones which they were as hooked on as a person suffering from emphysema was to their oxygen bottle.

What the tourists talked about had also changed. Back then, the foreigners who lived on the island talked about their travels, the continents they still wanted to explore and the wrongs that needed to be put right in the world. The expats who lived on the island these days were of an age where all they thought about was how to make the most of the years they had left. There were some young people amongst the strangers who visited the island. But when they weren't talking about a movie, gossiping about some movie star or comparing the number of "friends" they had on Facebook, they'd talk about their home town and their lives there with so much nostalgia and longing that all their travels seemed to do was make their home town and the work they did there — work which bored them the rest of year — all that much more interesting.

Basilius took out his notebook and pencil to jot down a few of these observations. As he did so, he realized they were the kind of cynical remarks he would have put into the mouth of his inspector.

"What's wrong?" Muriel asked when she heard him sigh.

"My brain is still in Levonian mode."

When they finally returned home, Muriel fed the stray cat she'd adopted, and then led her husband into the bedroom to take his mind off things.

Basilius followed her without much enthusiasm only because he didn't want to go back to his own room where he was sure Levonian was waiting for him.

But the bastard came to torment him in Muriel's bed.

"Poor woman," he said to his creator. "She probably thinks your cock is also in Levonian mode."

"Be patient," Basilius kept repeating to himself. "Inspiration can strike at any moment and when it does, he'll disappear for good."

-10-

T wo more weeks went by and not even the shadow of an idea had taken root in his mind.

So as not to disturb him, Muriel would leave every morning after breakfast and not come back until suppertime. Occasionally, she would stay for lunch at one or other of her new friends and she'd call her husband to tell him he was invited to join them. He would always decline saying he was writing. But when she got home at the end of the day, she never asked him about the work he was supposed to have done. No matter how hard Basilius tried to hide the anxiety that was overwhelming him, all it took was a glance and his wife could guess he hadn't written a word all day. So, instead, she'd tell him about her day.

"I ate at the Hungerford sisters. They're sixty-six years old and twins. From Scotland. I met them at the market. Their father is buried in the British military cemetery here on the island. They never knew him. He was killed by the Germans who occupied Nysa. That was before they were born. When they reached retirement, they decided to settle here and, once a week, they visit his grave, bring him flowers and recount another chapter of their lives to him. You should see their house — it's a real war museum with photos, maps, bayonets, bomb shells and everything. But their most precious "relic" has nothing to do with the Second World War."

Muriel showed him the picture of a small marble statue. It was the torso and upper thighs of a young ephebe.

"They wanted me to show this to you. According to them, the statue has to be from the sixth or seventh century BCE because the small arms are still joined to the body. They were so moved when they told me where and how they'd found it that they both had tears in their eyes."

During his first stay on Nysa, Basilius had spent the year walking all over the island without finding anything like this and so it was with a tinge of envy that he asked his wife where and how the two Scottish women had happened on this treasure.

"Their father died in the Bay of Pounta when the Allies landed there to liberate the island. So, the day after they arrived on Nysa, the two sisters went to see the place where he'd died and look for souvenirs of the battle. Naturally, after six decades, there was nothing left and they were getting ready to leave when they noticed a pebble in the sand with something carved on it. Think about it, Leo. More than a hundred generations of Nysians have walked that beach. For twenty-seven centuries, thousands of children have picked up pebbles and skipped them across the waves and fishermen have worked there day after day repairing their nets. And that's not counting the soldiers who fought on the beach. It's hard not to believe the statue was meant for them. They certainly do. They truly believe it's a gift from their father to make up for all the dolls and toys he was never able to buy them."

Muriel was trembling with emotion as she said this.

"You can keep the photo. But you mustn't talk to anyone about it. Unless you use it in your novel and if you do, you mustn't use their names. They don't want to get arrested for stealing an antique treasure. They're even convinced that there are people who wouldn't hesitate to kill them in order to steal the statue. That's why they've never shown it to anyone. Not even to Farley Marsh who knows a great deal about art and the Ancient Greeks and who could tell them all about where it comes from, its origins."

Every evening, Muriel would bring him home a story or two like this one in the hope that one of them might inspire her husband. If they were eating at a restaurant, one of Muriel's new friends might stop by their table for a chat. But Basilius would be about as talkative as the fish in his plate. This could be quite unsettling especially for people who liked to chat.

Once, however, the new acquaintance Muriel introduced him to — a man in his eighties by the name of Nicholas Laïos — wasn't satisfied with simply telling them some banal little tale and then moving on. He asked Basilius if he could sit down and join them and when Muriel requested that her husband listen to this man's story, he had no choice but to accept. Clearly, Muriel had told the man to come over and talk to him.

-11-

MANY PEOPLE HAD TOLD HIM their life story — or a part of it — in the hope that he would turn it into a book. He'd listen to them without saying a word. They'd leave when it became clear that their words were falling on deaf ears.

That's what he did that night. But it didn't impress Nicholas Laïos. He stopped talking only when he reached the end of his story.

Born on Nysa, he left the island at eighteen to do his military service. Then, he emigrated to the Belgian Congo where his uncle, his mother's brother, owned a restaurant. He married his first wife there and had his first child, a boy. Four years later, the rebels broke into his house one evening, attacking him and his wife with clubs and machetes. They threw his son out the window into the river that ran beside the house and then left to go kill other Whites, leaving him and his wife for dead.

But Nicholas Laïos survived. Only to realize he had lost everything he held dear in the world. All he had left were his eyes for crying.

After a few years of wandering — years during which he tried, twice, to take his own life — he ended up in Montreal, opened a restaurant, remarried and had a daughter who was thirty-eight today and worked for the government.

Nicholas Laïos recounted this in great detail and very dramatically. But still, it was a story like millions of others. Basilius, believing the old man had said everything he had to say, threw a sideward glance at his wife who said to him:

"Listen to the rest. I could've told you Nicholas' story myself, but I wanted you to hear it directly from him."

In a voice that was much more contained, the man continued.

"One morning, ten months ago, I'd just gotten out of bed when the phone rang at my house in Montreal. It was a call from Athens from the host of a television show that helps people find lost parents or friends. She wanted to know if I had lived in the Congo in the fifties and sixties. I told her I had. Do you remember a little boy called Procopis Laïos? she asked me. That was my son's name, the child the rebels had thrown to the crocodiles. So, I answered: Yes. Why are you asking me? By way of an answer all she said was: Do you have a parabolic antenna? Yes. Why all these questions? Watch my programme the day after tomorrow, she answered, and you'll have your answer. Oh, and, keep your phone close by."

Two days later, he turned on his television at the time she'd suggested.

The first guest was a man in his early fifties, white, born in the Congo, who spoke Greek with a Belgian accent. He said he was four years old when, during a night raid, the rebels killed his parents with clubs and machetes and threw him out the window into the river but he landed on the shore a few centimetres from the water. He got up and walked to the road in the dark. Cars were speeding by. White folk fleeing. A Belgian couple who ate at his father's restaurant recognized him. When he told them the rebels had killed his parents, they brought him to Belgium with them and adopted him without changing his name. They felt it was important he not forget his roots. When he finished university, they paid for a trip to Greece for him where he searched for someone who might have known his parents and who might have kept a picture of them. Eventually, he fell in love with a Greek woman, married her and got a job working in television. That's where, twenty years later, he met a Greek man from Montreal who said he knew a Nicholas Laïos who had lived in Africa.

When the phone finally rang at Nicholas' house, his wife answered: "My husband isn't able to speak," she told the TV host.

On the TV screen, Procopis Laïos, who had only hoped to find someone who could talk to him about his parents, was having as much difficulty speaking as Nicholas. He was barely able to tell Nicholas' wife that he'd be on the first flight out of Athens for Montreal the next day.

"Darling, look at my arm," Muriel said to her husband. "It's the second time I've heard this story and I still get goose bumps."

Nicholas Laïos' eyes were full of tears.

"The first thing to do, my wife said after the show, is a DNA test. Maybe he's an imposter, a con-man. A DNA test! I swear, Mr. Basilius, at the airport, when the customs gate opened, I knew with every fibre of my body that the man I was looking at was my flesh and blood. And he knew as well.

I'd seen him on television. But he didn't know what I looked like. There were about fifty people in the arrivals area, parents and friends who were there to meet passengers on the flight. But when they started coming through the gate, he came right over to me. We threw our arms around each other and both of us burst into tears … You can die peacefully now, Nico, I said to myself because you can't ask any more of life than this … There were one or two things left for me to do first. Go to Namur, in Belgium, to see the couple who had saved my son and kiss their hands and feet. That's done. After Namur, I came here to Nysa. I hadn't been back since I left for the Congo. Before dying, I wanted to rebuild my parents' house. For my son and for his son. My grandson is nineteen years old and his name is Nicholas like me."

He pulled a handkerchief out of his pocket and wiped his eyes.

"When your wife told me you were a writer and Canadian, like me, I said to myself: This is meant to be. It's the hand of fate. Again. A story like this, Mr. Basilius, has to be told. I'm sure you agree."

"I don't write biographies …"

"A novel, a play, an article, you decide. What's important is to tell the story. There are so many people who give up on life, Mr. Basilius. Twice. I tried to kill myself twice.

12

WHEN THE MAN HAD LEFT, Basilius said to his wife: "Never do something like that to me again. The poor man. He's so happy to have found his son after all these years, he won't give me a moment's peace until I've told his story to the entire world."

"I thought you wanted to write about the wonders and miracles of life —"

"That's not at all the kind of story I'm looking for."

"What are you looking for exactly?"

"I'll tell you when I find it."

Muriel emptied her glass and ordered another bottle of wine.

In Canada, she never had more than a glass of wine at dinner and never drank during the day. Now, when she got home from visiting her new friends, her cheeks were always a little rosy and her eyes sparkled. But Basilius never said a word. He was the one who had persuaded her to come here and he couldn't demand that, at her age, she spend her mornings jogging like Alicia and her afternoons exploring the seabed.

"Alright, but do you mind if I invite people over to the house?" Muriel said after a moment of silence. "You wanted me to make friends. And I've made friends who, one after the other, have invited me to lunch or dinner. I can't keep accepting their invitations without reciprocating. I leave you alone to write all day. Do you think you might, in turn, give me a day of your time without complaining and help me prepare brunch next Sunday? And, actually talk to my friends when they come to the house rather than stewing by yourself in a corner?"

Of course, Basilius said he would. But when they got home and Muriel had gone to bed, Levonian reappeared and said to him:

"Go back home, Leo. Not only does this island have nothing to offer you anymore but your wife is becoming an alcoholic."

With his eyes focussed on the dark expanse of the sea, Basilius ignored him.

But Levonian wouldn't leave him be. He paced around him the way he would a suspect in an interrogation room provoking, accusing, and threatening until he wore him down and broke him.

"Anyone can make a mistake. Happens to all of us. Your daily routine is stifling you and you want to make a change. Change where you live, your job, your life. Sometimes all it takes is a song. A song containing all the words you never use in real life. But you're a smart man and you should know that even if you succeed in throwing everything over so that you can finally say those words — say them and live them — you'll never be able to get away from yourself. From who you are. You're a writer of detective fiction, Leo, and you're too old to make yourself into something else. So, stop kidding yourself. Stop wasting your time following pipe dreams. You're too old for that. Once upon a time, the

39

smallest thing could dazzle you. The grey, miserable place you were in changed into a land of wonder. Every fisherman was picturesque, every café owner a real character, every sailor Ulysses. Because you didn't understand what they were saying to one another you missed the greed, the pettiness and the small-mindedness. You even idealized their poverty and saw it as poetic, as though, not unlike the hippies living on the island, it was by choice they turned their backs on our consumer society.

"In fact, when's the last time you read your poems and short stories? Maybe you should. You'll see that the beauty and light you came here to rediscover only existed in your head. The world, the real world, is a crock of shit, Leo, here and elsewhere. You've come to realize it for yourself now that the islanders speak better English. For sure, they didn't learn English in order to recite Homer or Sappho the way you thought they were doing years ago in Greek sipping a glass of ouzo. Or to get to know you better and *interact* with you like the painter of chairs claims they do. What more did Nicholas Laïos know about you after your meeting? He was interested in you for one reason only: to get you to talk about him in a book. But he won't even bother to read one of your novels. I'd bet my life on it.

"It's the same everywhere, Leo. Take people's dreams. A bigger television set, a bigger cock, bigger tits. Have you ever seen, here or at home, an ad for a bigger heart, a bigger brain? Even the hippies gave up on their dreams. Mortgages, pension plans and the stock exchange stifled their desires, their souls. And, now that age prevents them from escaping on acid trips, they console themselves with alcohol and Viagra. So, do yourself a favour and return to the detective novel, old man. At least it gives a true picture of humanity. You know it. Deep down inside, you know it."

By way of response, Basilius just shook his head and made his way back to his room to sleep.

13

HE SET ASIDE NOT JUST ONE but two days for Muriel's brunch. The first, he spent choosing the menu and shopping with his wife. The second, cooking and then mingling with their guests. He lost his temper only once when he snapped at Muriel and told her to stop repeating how much good all this was doing him and that he needed to get his mind off things.

Basilius' only concern was that the guests would want to talk to him about detective novels. Muriel tried to reassure him. She had specifically asked them not to and, in fact, once they arrived, they talked about all sorts of things, except crime fiction.

Basilius was unsettled by Alicia, however. She was not only the youngest and the most beautiful of all the guests but she was wearing a white linen dress with only a bikini string underneath. He could see her entire body outlined against the sun when she stood in front of him and said:

"I was brushing my teeth, last night, when from the bathroom window I saw a young man climbing the wall of the house next door — the house of an Austrian tenor who's lost his voice. The man slipped inside through the bedroom window. My first reaction was to yell "Thief!" but my mouth was full of toothpaste. As I was rinsing it, I had time to think.

If he really is a thief, I said to myself, why is he breaking in when the occupants are there? And if, on the other hand, he's a rapist and knows there's a woman sleeping in the room, he must also know she has a husband sharing her bed. Then, I remembered what the Austrian woman had told me about her husband. Since he lost his voice, he's also lost all interest in life and does nothing most of the time. Apparently, two or three evenings a week, he puts on his headphones and spends the entire night in the living room drinking and listening to recordings of his old recitals. That's probably what he was doing last night. Because, this morning, while he was sleeping off the wine and the melancholy, she was the one singing, happily, as she prepared her breakfast in the kitchen."

"It takes a woman to find something like that amusing," Drew said.

"What is she supposed to do? Ignore her desires and spend her nights mourning her husband's lost voice?" his sweetheart snapped back. "We're not in Afghanistan."

"Even in Afghanistan, nothing can stop a woman who's decided to cheat on her husband," said Tania, a woman in her 40's born in Nysa but now living in the States. "Have you read *The Burqa Seen from the Inside*? There's quite a racy story in it about a Taliban who was so jealous that when he went to work in the field, he never turned his back on his house in case another man tried to enter it. So, what did his wife do? She told her lover to visit when she was making bread and to hide in the privy which was behind the house. When the time was right, she called to her husband saying: 'My hands are covered in flour and dough, could you come and pull down my panties so I can go to the bathroom.' The husband came running, pulled up her burqa and lowered her panties.

43

Then, his wife went into the outhouse. The husband closed the door behind her and stood guard out front. She emerged ten minutes later and said to her husband: 'I'm done. You can lift my panties and pull down my burqa.'"

"Good for her!" Alicia said.

She was still silhouetted against the sun. Basilius could no longer pretend not to see her magnificent body. He got up and started refilling the Hungerford sisters' wine glasses. They were the oldest of the guests. And today they were both wearing silk dresses, identical except for the colour: pink for one, blue for the other. Everything matched — their shoes, their parasols, the flowers in their hair, even the reading glasses hanging from a cord around their necks. They looked like two young girls disguised as adults. Their voices even had the rhythms and the excitement of little girls when they asked Basilius if his wife had spoken to him about their father.

"Yes. She told me he died in the Bay of Pounta in 1944."

"Saturday, September 8th, at 6:30 in the morning," the twin in blue added.

"He was part of the Allied Amphibian Forces come to liberate the island," said the twin in pink.

"Under the command of Admiral Bernard Winterslow."

"Nysa had been occupied by the Germans since November, 1943."

"A battalion of the elite Brandebourg division, backed by twelve 88mm anti-aircraft guns and two giant Krupp cannons."

"The Germans had set up the giant cannons on the top of Mount Zarifi. From there they could hit an enemy ship at four thousand metres."

After years of research, they had done a complete reconstruction of the event and knew everything about the battle including the names of all the officers, German, Australian, Canadian and British who had taken part in the battle which had claimed their father's life — a father they had never known. They would have told him everything in detail, minute by minute, starting with their father's departure by convoy from Alexandria in Egypt up to his death in the Aegean fifty-two hours later except that Drew, who had either heard it all before or who had opinions about everything and had to add his two cents worth, said:

"Can you imagine what the population of the Earth would be today if there had never been any wars? It's the fashion, especially with artists who crave the spotlight, to deplore the harm people and nations do to one another and to entreat them to peace, love and forgiveness. But what will happen to the world now that we can no longer count on good old-fashioned epidemics and plagues to keep our numbers down? We're not going to be able to get by with only the occasional air plane crash, earthquake or tsunami every two or three years. Luckily, the Islamist don't give a hoot about what artists think or say. May Allah give them the nuclear know-how they covet! And soon too!"

"You are such an asshole sometimes!" Alicia sighed.

She picked up Muriel's kitten which had been rubbing up against her legs meowing and said to it:

"You can't stand to listen to any more of his bullshit either, can you?"

Inspector Levonian leaned in close to Basilius' ear and, pointing his index finger at Alicia, whispered:

"There's your next novel!

14

B ASILIUS IGNORED HIM. But Levonian could be very
stubborn when he got an idea in his head.

"I can't stand seeing you unhappy like this," he said. "So
here's what I'm thinking: If you don't want to go back home
to Canada, bring me over to Nysa. With that nice little ass
of hers and her beautiful long legs, tailing Alicia would be
a real pleasure. Look at her. Little pussy here, little pussy
there. Why do you think she keeps repeating it as she pats
the kitten in her lap? And all those references to the wife of
the tenor? Start using your little grey cells, Leo. Why do you
think she told us about the wife of the tenor and cheered for
the Afghan woman? It certainly wasn't to titillate her man.
He's too preoccupied with the post-modern novel to spend
any time lingering over his girlfriend's little bush. That's
why she was so pissed off the other night at the méchoui.
Everyone thought our lovebirds arrived late because they'd
had sex on the beach and then fallen asleep exhausted and
satisfied. Everyone except you and me. You've gotta have
flair, Leo. And clues. You've got to be able to sniff 'em out.
The clues. And my sniffer tells me that this isn't going to
end well. Unless she finds a man — and soon. A real man
who can release the frustration that's been building in her all
through these hot, lazy summer days perfect for the cult of

the body, if you get my meaning. Otherwise, her frustration will build and set off some kind of violent, savage, act. You can take my word for it. One hot, sweltering night, fed up of being debauched only with words, our beautiful Alicia will run amok and smash her man's head in and then insist the asshole fell on it running after an idea."

"Picture the interrogation scene with moonlight, crickets. The works. A tough interrogation. Tough, in-depth and very long. To wear down her resistance. You could even use the twins and work out a B-story around that statue of theirs. There's something Freudian in all that. I'm sure of it. Okay, now, cutting to the chase, the painter sends the two old birds to join their father, grabs the statue and claims he's the one who found it: a gift from the gods telling him he's on the right track with his stupid chairs. To spice things up, you could also bring in the tenor, his wife and her toy-boy. Finally, to make Muriel happy, you can throw in something about the old guy who found his kid after fifty years.

"Stop racking your brain for ideas. It's all there. Your next novel. And a lot sexier than those fancy ideas of yours. They're enough to put anyone to sleep. I come out of my coma. To recuperate and get my health back, I come here and end up solving a murder or two. I deserve an adventure by the sea. A change of scene, the sun, the sea and some fresh air will do me a world of good.

"Oh God! Did you see how she moves her leg when she hugs the cat in her lap? Do you think it excites her? Maybe she's having an orgasm? The poor child! Having to satisfy herself with a quickie and a cat … But why's she doing it in public? Now? Definitely not to excite the two queens she's staying with. They're even less interested in little pussies

47

than her looser of a boyfriend. Well, well, well, she just glanced up to see if you're looking at her.

"Goddammit, do something!"

Levonian, usually so laconic, wouldn't stop egging him on. Like some kind of match-maker.

"I'm sure she wore that see-through dress and talked about the wife of the tenor just for you. Poor thing, she thinks you made me in your image and all it takes is a pair of string panties to get you excited. Oh, if I could touch her, I'd've trimmed her little bush a long time ago, believe me."

Basilius stared at him, astonished. Levonian was known for his sharp, acidic humour. His frank, direct way of speaking only added to his charm. But he was never vulgar. What had come over him suddenly?

"It's the sun, the sea, bare thighs everywhere and that pussycat in the middle of it all. I promise you I'll go back to being true to my character again and I won't say anything I'm not supposed to say as soon as I start a new investigation."

How many times had he told him there wouldn't be another investigation? But Levonian wouldn't drop it. He even suggested that Leo should make himself, the writer, a character in his next crime story.

"Apparently, auto-fiction is very much the fashion these days. There's a huge demand for washing your dirty laundry in public. So … how about this? A writer at a loss for inspiration kills his aging wife thinking a pretty young thing with gorgeous legs will do wonders for his testosterone and his imagination. Unless … wait! I've got it! It's his young disciple overcome with admiration for the King of Crime who gets rid of his wife for him? Or her frigid boyfriend who does her in when he discovers she's been fooling around with a guy who's more famous and talented than he is?

"Oh look, she's getting up … she's coming over to you! And you can be sure it's not to ask you for an autograph. Not rolling her hips and ass like that. She must've said to herself: Maybe the great Basilius is short-sighted. Maybe I should shove my nice titties under his nose."

"Mr. Basilius, I've noticed when I'm out jogging in the morning that you like to get up early too."

She bent down towards him sending sweet waves of her body smells in his direction. She lowered her voice and added:

"I don't want Drew to hear me. He'd want to come along and would spoil everything with his insipid remarks."

She went on to explain that the tradition in the Greek Orthodox religion is to dig up the bones of the deceased after three years, wash them with wine and then place them in the family vault. That was why Tania had come to Nysa from the United States. She was supposed to dig up her father's bones the next morning and had invited Alicia to the ceremony.

"I thought you might like to join us."

He had come to Nysa to think about life not death. But Levonian wouldn't leave him be: "Accept the invitation," he said. "A breath of fresh air like her will help to clear your head. It's exactly what you need. And the visit to the cemetery could inspire a scene for the book."

Basilius accepted her invitation if only to shut the detective up.

Alicia, delighted he'd be joining them, said she'd pick him up the next morning at five o'clock. Levonian stood there watching them with a sly smile on his face. The kind of smile that said he knew exactly how things were going to play out.

"So, feeling any better?" Muriel asked him when the guests had left and he was helping her wash up and put things away.

Basilius said he was. Their guests had helped clear his head. He also told her about Alicia's invitation and asked whether she'd like to come along with them.

"Get up with the birds to watch a body being dug up and bones being washed? It would depress me for the rest of the day."

-15-

ALL IT TOOK WAS ONE WORD, a single word, to produce the spark he was hoping for. Basilius heard it the next morning among the gravestones.

It was an unbelievably ordinary word uttered in the most incongruous circumstances imaginable.

Alicia picked him up at five o'clock on the dot. She was driving a Vespa and wearing a loose flowing black dress which revealed nothing of her body underneath.

"I love this time of day," she said while he settled on the scooter behind her. "I love the silence when I jog at dawn. I feel as though I'm the only person on the island. I can say something like this to you. Drew would laugh at me."

Then she grabbed his hands and, without any shyness or suggestiveness, placed them firmly on her waist.

"Hang on tight. The road is full of hair-pin turns and you could fall off in one of the bends."

The contact of their hands immediately called up the image of the cat she had caressed in her lap the day before. To drive the image from his mind, he thought of his daughter who was the same age as Alicia. He told himself that the waist he was holding was hers.

"Do you jog every morning?" he asked to show her that the contact of their bodies wasn't the only thing he was thinking about.

"Yes, except for Sundays. After jogging I go for a swim in a little creek. There's never anybody there at that hour and I like to swim in the nude before the sun starts to really get hot."

"What do you do the rest of the day?" he asked immediately to show her that the word "nude" had had no effect on him.

"I write. I'm writing a novel. My first."

He prayed she wouldn't ask him to read her manuscript. Over the years, many young people had asked him for advice. He enjoyed helping them. But not anymore. He didn't have it in him anymore to concern himself about other people's first literary steps. Alicia didn't mention her book again and he was grateful for that.

The sky was still dark. But by the time they had made the climb up to the cemetery, the first rays of sunlight had started to break through.

In the cemetery, two little boys were running around between the graves while the gravedigger, standing in a hole he had dug, was picking up bones and handing them to Tania and her mother, an elderly woman dressed entirely in black. The two women washed the bones with wine and then put them in a box lined with midnight-blue satin while a little girl watched them a deep frown on her face.

"That's Jenny, my eldest," Tania told Basilius. "She loves reading."

Then, she turned to the girl:

"Mr. Basilius is a writer. He writes books."

But, at that moment, the little girl was more interested in the skull the gravedigger had just handed to her grandmother who was looking at it intently, her chin trembling.

"They lived and worked together for forty-three years," Tania said to Basilius and Alicia.

The old woman, who didn't understand a word of English, washed the skull gently as though it was still covered with flesh. When she was finished, she called her two grandsons over to see what was left of their grandfather, a man they had never known. But the two boys preferred to throw rocks at the cypress trees that the birds squawking and crying transformed into a world full of sound and life as the first rays of the sun touched the highest branches and painted the sky pink.

"I'm going to pick some flowers to put in the box with Grampy," the girl said to her mother.

She had hardly taken two steps when she stopped stock-still as a rooster's cry suddenly broken the silence.

"Mom ..."

"What, sweetie?

"Why does the rooster sing every morning?

"Ask Mr. Basilius. He'll know better than me. He's a writer."

During his thirty-year career, Basilius had had to answer questions from journalists, professors and students, fans and detractors, even chiefs of police and politicians. Not once had he been caught up as short as that morning, in the cemetery, when the little girl turned to him and said:

"Mr. Basilius, why does the rooster sing every morning?"

He could've answered that the rooster was announcing the arrival of dawn to a sleeping world with his song. Or something like that. But now that he was forced to actually think about it, that answer didn't satisfy him. He was searching for another one when, like a *deus ex macchina*, the priest providentially arrived to save him. He invited everyone to follow him to the chapel with the bones of the deceased.

In the chapel, the bones were laid out on a small table, in front of the iconostasis. The priest burnt incense and swung the burner over the bones as he recited a few prayers. When he'd finished, the bones were returned to the box and the box was placed in the family vault. Then, the deceased's wife offered everyone biscuits "for my husband's soul". They made their way home while traffic picked up on the streets, lanes and roads of the island. But Basilius registered none of this, or hardly. Even when he sat back down behind Alicia on the Vespa, the contact of their two bodies had no effect on him at all. And when the young woman dropped him at his house, he thanked her with a distracted air.

If the little girl had quickly forgotten her question, impressed by the Mass for the Dead, all Basilius could think about was roosters and their song.

-16-

H E SPENT THE DAY in front of his laptop searching the Internet for a study, a folk tale, a story, an article, anything that dealt with the song of the rooster. He even called one of his friends who was a veterinarian and another who was an expert in folklore and myths. Both confirmed what he had already deduced from his research on the Net that since time immemorial and all around the world, it was thought that the rooster sang in the morning to herald the dawn.

He wasn't doing all this just to satisfy the curiosity of a little girl of seven. The spark he had experienced was exactly like the ones he had had many times before when a word overheard or read by chance suddenly led him out of the impasse his writing had led him into. That said, some sparks — the "bad good-ideas" he liked to call them — had led him down paths where he had lost considerable amounts of time. After all, he had been hearing the rooster crow every morning for the last month without it making any impression on him. So why was it sparking his interest now? If it was out of desperation, sooner or later, he'd lose interest and come to regret the hours he had spent on it. Besides, this wasn't the kind of story he was used to writing or even close to the subject of the novel he wanted to write. So, even though his gut instinct told him to pursue the cock's-crow lead, he threw his notes away and decided not to think about it anymore.

But the question kept coming back to him as persistent as an earworm you can't stop no matter how hard you try. It was as though, coming from a child, the question took on a whole different significance from the one adults gave it.

"Why does the rooster sing every morning?"

His instinct told him this might be "the candle". The candle was a metaphor he'd used in one of his crime novels and put in the mouth of the main character. Levonian was talking about how he went about solving a case and the words and images he used were directly inspired by Basilius' own process when he was plotting a new novel.

> *I find myself in a building I'm not familiar with. I have to draw a plan of the place but the building is plunged in darkness. I try to find a light switch by feeling my way along the wall. Suddenly, my hand happens on a candle. I pick it up and continue to look, still groping in the dark. Eventually, I find a book of matches. I light the candle and by the light of its flame, at last, I find the light switch. I blow out the candle and now, with the light on in the room, I'm able to find the light switch for the next room and the next and the next until the whole building is ablaze with light.*

What if the little girl's question was the candle which would help him find the light switch and once the house was completely lit, he could either keep the candle or throw it away the way he had in the past? All his novels started with a murder. This new one would start with a song. The idea that the inciting incident would be the song of the rooster really appealed to him. He was convinced that with its cock-a-doo-dle-doo, cocorico, kukuruyuk, ake-e-ake-ake, u-urru-urru or whichever phonetic transcription of its song you prefer, the rooster didn't sing each morning to announce the coming of the dawn to sleeping humans or to tell them what time it was. That would be like saying chickens lay eggs for the sole purpose of feeding human beings and providing them with the protein, vitamin A and phosphorous they needed.

And so, he continued to ponder his dilemma — whether to pursue the idea of the rooster's song for a few more days or move on and look for something else. And it was precisely at that moment that Levonian re-appeared. He stood behind him, looked over his shoulder reading his notes and then burst out laughing.

"I send him to the cemetery with Alicia and he thinks he's with Alice in Wonderland! Tell me you're not planning on writing children's stories now, Leo. I'm going to start thinking you've really inherited your father's Alzheimer's."

Offended, Basilius answered: "I would gladly make a deal with the Devil and give up any last vestiges of lucidity I might have if, in exchange, he inspired me with a story as unique and immortal as Lewis Carroll's."

Any hint of laughter or teasing disappeared from Levonian's face.

"Why didn't you kill me off at the end of *Lost Lights*?" he asked his creator. "Your novels are implacably logical. From the first page to the last, not a superfluous or arbitrary word. Every gesture and every line of dialogue has been thought through. So, tell me this: If you were so determined to abandon crime fiction forever, why didn't you kill me off at the end of *Lost Lights*?"

"I thought about it. The idea made me sick, physically."

"You've killed hundreds of people. Children even."

"That was different. You and I co-habited for thirty-four years. Shared the same torments, the same joys. You were my most faithful companion. I couldn't kill you. And especially not at the hands of a psychopath!"

"Give me a break! You wanted to keep the door open. In case you weren't able to write anything else."

Basilius shook his head.

"I will never return to the crime novel. Never."

"That's gratitude for you! He says I was his most faithful companion and, while I was doing everything I could to catch his psychopath, he was plotting my disappearance. Am I supposed to feel grateful that I'm in a coma?

"You should've let me die, Leo. I have projects too, you know. And I'm more determined than you are to see them through. If yours really mattered to you, you would've left your wife in Canada. Imagine all the amazing things a young woman like Alicia could've helped you discover. Muriel wouldn't get up at five in the morning to see Atlantis rise from the sea. But, with Alicia, the two of you could've gone swimming naked in the little creek after her jogging and then hand-in-hand you would've watched the sun come up and marvelled at the rosy fingered dawn, as you talked about the rooster's song, extolling the beauty of the world and the virtues of humankind, dreaming about a future without evil, crime and war, and — why not? — without hurricanes or earthquakes either. Oh, Alicia would've made you see so many wonderful things. If you really believed in your dream, Leo, you'd send Muriel back to Canada today. You've made dozens of women cry and die for a lot less. Get rid of yours so you can write your masterpiece in peace. But truth be told, in real life, you have about as much balls as I have tits. And that's why, of the two of us, I'm the one who's going to come out of this the winner. So, do yourself a favour. Stop this nonsense and come back to the crime novel. You've wasted enough time counting the waves."

"Don't answer," Basilius said to himself. "Concentrate on the little girl's question. Don't say another word to him."

TWO WEEKS LATER, he still hadn't found anything.

He'd get up at dawn, settle on the terrace with a cup of coffee facing the Levant. The roosters crowed, the sun rose, the hours went by and he cursed the morning he had followed Alicia to the cemetery because, try as he may, he couldn't seem to find the match which would light the candle. All he got out of these musings were migraines and backache.

He wanted to start over at the beginning, pursue a new idea, on more familiar ground. But he had this stupid question about the rooster in his head and — he knew what he was like, the same as his detective — he'd have to see it through to the end and resolve the mystery of the cock's crow before he could bury it for good.

Then, there was the cat his wife had adopted. Whenever Basilius spotted the damn animal he'd remember what Levonian had said about Muriel: He wouldn't succeed in freeing himself totally from his past as a writer of detective novels until he got away from the woman who had been his life companion for the past thirty-five years. And, when he saw Alicia jogging by in the morning and she waved to him, he wondered why she'd told him that after her run she swam naked in the little creek.

"I can tell *you*."

Why had she added that? Was it because he liked to get up at the crack of dawn like her? Had she read the short story he'd written inspired by a little creek on Nysa?

Now you're going too far, Leo. Concentrate on the little girl's question!

He wanted to, but the damn cat, as though it was in cahoots with Levonian to get him involved in an affair which would reek havoc with his marriage and his new writing project, kept coming around rubbing against his leg. Meow, it seemed to be saying, Alicia is waiting for you, naked, in the little creek, just like Loraine did all those years ago.

"The poor little cat," Muriel said one day when she saw her husband send the kitten flying with a kick. "It's not its fault if you're not getting anywhere with your novel."

That night, made bold by Muriel's love, the dirty little beast pursued Basilius into his bed and his dreams.

"The pussy is also part of the beauty of the world and one of the wonders of life," said Alicia's voice on the telephone. "Pat it a little. To show you love it."

There was a soft rumbling sound, gentle but amplified, as if the phone was being rubbed against a hairy surface.

"Yes, that's right, yes," Alicia's voice said. "Can you hear it purring? Don't stop!"

When he opened his eyes to escape from this troubling dream and its inevitable conclusion, the damn cat was rolled up in a ball, purring, inches from his face.

Basilius grabbed it by the scruff of the neck, threw it out of the room and slammed the door. Five minutes later, he realized that without air conditioning or a draft, the room had become a lot stuffier.

Re-opening the door was out of the question. Instead he took the screen off the window to allow more air to circulate. Then, to fend off the mosquitos and the bad dreams that were lying in wait ready to pounce, he took one of Muriel's sleeping pills. Levonian watched him with a wry smile, the kitten perched on his left shoulder and his eyes twinkling in the half darkness.

"There's only one way to get rid of a cat," he said. "But, in real life, you haven't even got what it takes to drown a kitten."

He's right, Basilius thought as he laid back down on the bed with an arm covering his eyes. I have something to say. Something simple. Something I want to say in a different, original way to help bury the wickedness we all carry inside us. But, I'm a fine one to talk. I'm the one who can't seem to bury anything.

-18-

MURIEL HAD NEVER SEEN her husband looking so overwhelmed and so discouraged. Of course, there'd been times when he hit a wall in the course of his writing, but he knew how to make a story work and was always able to solve the problem after a few days. This time was different. He seemed more lost now than three months earlier when he'd told her he wanted to go to Nysa to write because he couldn't seem to get his new project off the ground.

"Nothing's working?" she asked him. "Are you stuck?"

"Since we arrived here, I've seen and heard enough to write a new novel in six months."

"You should write it, then. Put everything into it you never wrote about in your other books. It could be a joyful crime novel, full of light, especially if you set it on the shores of the Aegean in the middle of summer."

Levonian reappeared to throw in his two cents' worth.

"She's right. Publishers don't like books that leave the beaten track. And readers don't like to change their reading habits. You must've noticed: They prefer repetition to something new."

So now the cop thinks he's some kind of literary critic. Basilius wanted to tell Levonian he didn't need his two-bit insights but he couldn't do it in front of his wife. Instead, he kept his eyes on Muriel and, hoping to shut Levonian up once and for all, he said:

"Whether the new crime novel is dark or joyful, in twenty or thirty years it'll be forgotten like all my other detective novels."

"Did Drew's high-falutin' theories about the fleeting success of crime fiction put those ideas into your head?"

"No. I've thought it for years."

"Why didn't you ever talk to me about it?"

Because it was so vain. It made him blush to think about it. And blush he did when at last he admitted to his wife that he hadn't given up writing detective fiction because he wanted to write about the beauty of the world and its light. He had another motive. A motive that had been tormenting him ever since it entered his mind and his heart. A desire so strong, so obsessive that not a single novel he'd written since then, no matter how good, had succeeded in satisfying it. It was the reason why he'd decided to stop writing crime fiction. Before he died or lost his mind, he wanted to write something he'd never attempted to write before, something unique, something that didn't exist before him, something that would pass down to posterity and guarantee the immortality of his body of work and of his name. But no matter how hard he tried he couldn't come up with the one idea that would help him win the race he was running against the overwhelming silence of oblivion. On an island bathed in sunlight, he felt more and more as though he was coming and going in a fog.

"But I refuse to give up," he concluded. "I might as well admit I've ruined my life."

Levonian hung his head as though, finally, he understood he'd lost. But Basilius didn't have the time to enjoy his victory. Muriel, rather than sympathizing with her husband, bridled at his words and with bitterness in her voice said:

"For a poor woman like me who doesn't calculate her worth based on the distance that separates her from the pantheon of the great, there's nothing more demoralising than to see yourself diminished in the eyes of the man you love. I'm not saying that because you hid the real reason for giving up crime fiction from me. You're free to write whatever you want. I say it because you truly believe that your life would be a failure if your plan for immortality doesn't succeed. It's as if I didn't count or the three children we had together or their children, your grandchildren. None of us count in your eyes as much as a single page of some masterpiece which is supposed to guarantee your immortality."

"I was talking about my writing life …"

"When you talk about your life, you only talk about yourself as a writer! I know that and I've accepted it. You prefer to engage with your keyboard than with a human being. Not only have I accepted it but I always try to accommodate it and offer you the peace and quiet you need in order to work. I cared for the children and my varicose veins without disturbing you in your "lair" with the hundred and one small daily problems I had to deal with. I only go to you once in a blue moon with my problems or those of one of the children. An example: Your daughter has been calling me every day for the past two weeks. If she was a character in one of your novels, you would've done everything you could to find out why. But you prefer not to ask in case the answer might disturb your literary musings."

"How could I have asked if you didn't tell me she was calling every day because you didn't want to disturb me in my "lair"?

"You see? I did tell you! But you never listen to me. You should've come to Nysa alone, Leo. Ever since you've started to hear the call of the sirens of posterity, I get the impression my voice has become background noise, like the cicadas or the cat."

The kitten was rubbing up against Muriel's legs as she said this.

"To you, this is just meowing. But the cat doesn't meow just for the pleasure of going meow, meow. It's trying to say something. What are you trying to tell me, puss? Are you hungry?"

Basilius grabbed his pen and, with fingers suddenly full of energy again, he wrote the following sentence in his notebook: "What is it saying?" He underlined it twice. His face had lit up as though this short sentence had burned off the fog that had settled around him.

His wife shook her head and, then, with the kitten following close on her heels, she made her way towards the kitchen saying:

"My heart is in tatters. I tell him his daughter has been calling every day and, rather than ask me why, he makes notes for his goddam novel!"

-19-

THE CREATIVE PROCESS works in mysterious ways. Basilius was in the depths of despair, his wife accused him of egotism and insensitivity and all it took was an ordinary observation about something as far removed from what was preoccupying him as a cat is from a rooster, to spark his imagination again.

"The cat doesn't meow for the pleasure of meowing. It's trying to say something."

It was so logical, so simple really, that he couldn't understand why he hadn't thought of it before.

"Why does the rooster sing every morning? What's it saying?"

That's how he should've phrased the question instead of drowning in a sea of hypothetical theories one more convoluted and absurd than the other. Because, in point of fact, the rooster doesn't sing. For Basilius, a human being, it's a song. But for the rooster, it's a language. Words that express a thought, a need, a feeling.

"Don't get carried away" he reasoned after he'd jotted these notes down in his notebook. "This isn't the match you were looking for. It's only the candle. You'll find the match once you've answered the question: What is the rooster trying to say when it crows in the morning? The answer will light the candle and allow you to find the first light switch."

He also wrote down Muriel's comment about the children and varicose veins — when you're working on a novel, you never know what will be of use — then, his face glowing with renewed hope and energy, he walked into the kitchen, showed his notebook to his wife and said:

"I wasn't thinking about my project, my love. I wrote: 'What did she say?' to remind myself to ask you, once you'd stopped tearing a strip off me, why Clara was calling every day."

Muriel wasn't wearing her reading glasses and couldn't see that the personal pronoun in the sentence he was showing her wasn't "she" but "it".

Levonian had noticed however.

"You're a real shit!" he said to his creator. "And I can't even grab you and make you take back the bullshit you're spewing. I'm supposed to be virtue personified. Believe me, I'll find a way. Do you hear me? I'm not going to let myself be buried by a rooster!"

Ignoring him, Basilius asked Muriel why their daughter was calling every day.

"She just broke up with her boyfriend," his wife answered. "Good riddance! I could never stand the jerk. But she loves him and spends her days crying. Would it bother you if I invited her to come spend a few weeks here? It would take her mind off things."

Levonian's vexation suddenly turned into a sardonic grin while the joy Basilius had been feeling because he'd succeeded in reformulating his question changed into annoyance.

68

It was Clara's fourth separation in ten years. The three other times, she'd moved back in with her parents and spent her days dragging herself around the house sighing and monopolizing everyone with her tale of woe. He wouldn't be able to put up with it. Not this time. Even if he got her a room in a hotel — something Muriel would definitely not agree to — she'd spend her days at their house interrupting her father's work with her tears and lamentation. It might've disturbed him less if he'd been more advanced in his project. But he hadn't even found what the book was about yet and, at the moment, with no other lead, all he wanted to do was pursue the idea of the rooster and its song.

Basilius didn't dare say any of this out loud. Hadn't his wife just accused him of being egotistical and insensitive? All he did was suggest they wait a few days before inviting their daughter to Nysa. Who knows, Clara and her boyfriend might get back together. It had happened before.

In order to help Muriel forget about their daughter's separation and to gain a few brownie points, that night he took her out to the taverna where her new friends ate. And when they got back home, he was the one who took his wife to bed, to *his* bed, to take her mind off things. He had one idea in mind: before his daughter arrived, find out what the rooster was saying when it sang every morning. Once he did, his project would be off and running.

-20-

THE NEXT DAY, Basilius got up and left the house while it was still dark. He wanted to arrive at a henhouse he'd spotted on the outskirts of town before the rooster crowed.

Six chickens and one rooster were inside an enclosure two metres by three surrounded by a chain link fence. When Basilius got there, the chickens and the rooster were poking around, pecking at the ground looking for food. There was also a rat in the enclosure. He was gorging himself on the grain thrown down for the poultry. But the chickens didn't pay attention to the rodent anymore than they did to Basilius. Even the rooster, an animal known for its sense of territory and its combativity, ignored the rat rather than fight it.

Basilius had never been curious about hens and roosters and if someone had asked him what he was looking for he would've had a hard time answering.

He was observing.

Observing in the hope that at some point certain details would come together and make sense to him. He was looking for a meaning other than the one generally ascribed to the song of the rooster. Because, if Basilius was sure of one thing, it was that the rooster's song wasn't announcing the arrival of dawn or that the hens had just laid fresh eggs. Like Muriel's kitten, as long as it had food to eat, the rooster couldn't care less if human beings knew that it was the beginning of a new day or that the hens had just laid fresh eggs.

The rooster was a magnificent creature. From the top of its red cockscomb all the way to the tip of its tail feathers, its colours were breathtaking. But what was most impressive was the way it carried its head with such an air of assurance and dignity.

It wasn't surprising to Basilius that for certain cultures the rooster was associated with courage, pride and haughtiness and its cry interpreted as an expression of arrogance.

But courage aside, all these attributes were exclusively human. And now that, for once, he had the opportunity to open a novel with a song, Basilius wasn't going to ruin or pervert that song and the bird singing it with human feelings and pretty loathsome ones at that.

After some thought, he realized he couldn't attribute courage to the rooster either. If it was brave, why did it retire to its perch as soon as darkness fell and then, like a common sparrow, not make a sound all night long?

Fear of predators bigger and stronger than it was?

The rooster knew that no predator could reach it in its enclosure.

Fear of the dark then?

In which case, the song the rooster finally sang at dawn could only be one of relief or joy. And like fear and anguish, joy as an emotion was not exclusively human.

"So, to sum up," Basilius said to himself.

Every night, a prisoner of darkness, the rooster is filled with anguish. Could this be the end? the rooster wonders.

All night long, it prays for the return of the sun to chase away the darkness so it can live, eat, and copulate once more.

Suddenly, it crows.

If the rooster had crowed while it was still night, it would've been a prayer. Something along the lines of: Sun, bring joy back to me!

But the rooster hadn't crowed yet.

So, it only crows when it feels the day dawning.

And it follows that the cock's crow can only be one thing — an explosion of joy.

At the sight of the first rays of dawn.

Of life returning.

Quickly, Basilius pulled out his notebook and pen to write all this down before he forgot it. And especially, before the rooster started singing. That's what he came here for: to observe the cock while it sang.

But he'd barely written the last letter of the last word when Levonian, who had appeared behind him and had read his notes over his shoulder, said:

"Oh! You hypocrite! You shit!"

-21-

WITH THE RELENTLESSNESS he brought to everything he did, once he'd started, Levonian couldn't stop vilifying Basilius.

"He doesn't want to pervert the rooster's song by ascribing base human feelings to it," he said, "but in order to carve a place for himself in the eyes of posterity, he puts his most loyal companion into a coma. You can fool everyone with this business about the rooster's song, Leo, but not me. I'll return every day to remind you of your betrayal and all the vices you've so carefully hidden behind the mask of a sage. How, for instance, you created men and women for the sole purpose of ruining their lives and came in your knickers when one of your creatures was tortured or raped."

Basilius had focused all his attention on the rooster convinced that as soon as he'd figured out the meaning of its song, Levonian would disappear. But when he heard that last slanderous insult, he couldn't stop himself from shouting:

"That's not true!"

"Then why did you spend the best years of your life making up all those disgusting things if you didn't get off on them? You were young, healthy, good natured and happy. And yet, you spent your days creating a deeply disturbing world and showing nothing but the depravity of the human soul. Why? Unless you were hiding your true nature under a pleasant exterior while you secretly enjoyed the smell of blood and of burning flesh?"

"I didn't just show the depravity of the human soul. You're a good example of that. And not the only one either. Be honest."

"Then, how come, in sixteen novels, I wasn't happy for even one whole chapter?"

"That's not true!"

"I had a few happy moments, I'll admit, but you ended them as soon as you could with some misfortune."

"You're not being fair, Levonian."

"Okay. Refresh my memory then. Give me one example of a time when I was living my life happily and some kind of misfortune didn't come along after a few pages to darken everything. You're not saying anything? That's because there aren't any. Novel after novel, there was nothing on the horizon for me but horror. That was my fate. As soon as I wrapped up one investigation, you'd drop me into yet another gruesome location cordoned off with yellow tape where death had struck. And it would start all over again. Question the local cops the first to arrive on the scene. Talk to the coroner and crime scene technicians. Gather witness statements. Break the bad news to the family. Question the victim's friends and colleagues. Climb stairs. Knock on doors which would open to reveal hardship, drama and sometimes even a gun. Because people don't like cops. If some of them are content to complain when they're disturbed at home, others dream of shooting us. The rest of the time, you had me going through drawers and closets, examining clothes and small personal objects that might reveal the character and proclivities of a victim or a suspect or checking out the toilets of crack houses that hadn't been cleaned since the day they were installed. Then there were the stake-outs and the surveillances, doing the rounds of informers and other losers whose only goal in life was to come up with a brilliant scheme that would guarantee they'd make a million bucks without doing a day's work. Always the same questions and always on the alert for a hesitation, the trembling of a lip or a change of tone which could signal a lie or a deliberate omission. Be patient, I'd say to myself. Someone's got to do the job."

"And you did it so well that your investigations made you famous the world over. Thanks to the movies, even people who don't read know who you are, but have no idea who I am."

"It wasn't a popularity contest, Leo. When I'd speed down a street pedal to the metal, light flashing on the roof of the car, siren screaming, it wasn't to show off but to do my duty in good conscience like the taxpayers asked me to do. Up until my last case, that is. After spending thirty years with the dregs of society, I thought I'd seen everything and nothing could shock me. But when I walked into that pedophile's apartment, when I saw all his sadistic paraphernalia and the little mutilated bodies … Enough, I said to myself. It's time to hand in my badge and deal with my own pain and suffering … That's what I was supposed to do, yes or no?"

"Yes …"

"So why am I in a coma, ruing the day I popped into your head for the first time? Is that the paradise you promised me as a reward for all my hard work and loyal service?

Thirty years dealing with death. Why isn't it me letting out a cry of joy as I watch the sun come up on a new day?"

Basilius was moved. This time, rather than turn his back on him, he answered him gently.

"Vass, I never promised you paradise. I don't even believe there is one."

"You taught me every word that comes out of my mouth. You put every thought I think into my head. Every hope and dream as well. After thirty years of loyal service, at last I'm going to get what's rightfully coming to me far from this hell-hole of bricks and cement that's always plunged in winter darkness. We talked about it every day at the police station. The blue paradise of retirement in Florida or the Caribbean. Every policeman's dream."

"I used the term with derision."

"It was a joke? There's no blue paradise either? It doesn't exist?"

"No, it's real. But all the cops who've been there … Look, they complain about how hard their lives are as cops and count the days until retirement. But when they finally get their freedom, they don't know what to do with it and, after six months of grand-daddy retirement with nothing else to worry about except sunburns and mosquitos, they can't stand the palm trees and the blue sea anymore and they beg to go back and serve. Again. Even for free. Remember Lieutenant Stewart …"

"I don't give a fuck about Stewart. The blue paradise is the only dream I have left. I think I deserve to at least go and see what it's like for myself. Read a book sitting by the water. Plant some flowers. Dance. Explore other sides of my personality. After always doing the same things over and over again, I feel like a donkey, always drudging down the same road, doing the same jobs, subjected to the same sorrows and the same worries. I'm not a donkey! In the years I have left, I want to laugh, travel, see the good side of life. You've been holding that dream out to me like a carrot for the last thirty years. Time to keep your promise. You can write whatever you want afterwards."

That was exactly when the rooster crowed its long-awaited cock-a-doodle-doo.

"**F**UCK!" Basilius muttered.

He'd come to see the rooster at the moment it crowed. But when he turned and looked at it, the bird had already stopped and was staring at the horizon flushed now with Homeric splendour.

The hens were also standing stock still and looking in that direction.

The rat continued to eat. Further off a goat was grazing tied to a post. A few sparrows were chirping as they gorged themselves in a fig tree.

Only the rooster and the hens were facing East staring with their eyes open wide.

Why?

It couldn't be because they had short memories and watched the sun come up every morning as if they were seeing it for the first time. If that were the case, the other animals, or at least their cousins, the sparrows, blackbirds and crows, would be just as intrigued or dazzled.

"To sum up," Basilius said to himself. "The rooster sings when the sky starts to grow pale. And when at last the sun rises, the rooster and the hens look at it with surprise.

"Because they think it's the rooster's song that made the sun rise?

"Is that where the rooster's pride comes from as well as its power over the hens?"

In the enclosure, the hens had started scratching the ground again, cackling and shaking their tails while the rooster walked among them with its head held high.

Basilius thought to himself: "I could swear the rooster thinks it's his song that ended the night and filled the sky with light. I can't fly, it seems to be saying to the hens, but I can dispel the darkness and bring you the light. Like countless priests and shamans who, for centuries, calculated at what time the sun rose every morning and made innocent people believe that with their prayers and incantations they had the power to lead them out of the darkness into the light. Not surprising some had made the rooster a religious symbol of faith and hope while others associated it with the idea of nationhood and the birth of a new era. Kings had incorporated the cock in their coats of arm."

While Basilius was pondering all this, the rooster jumped a hen and took her from behind.

Basilius looked down at his notebook and scribbled some of these thoughts. He was convinced that the rooster's song wasn't so much a prayer as a song of victory.

But when the sun had come up, rather than bragging, the rooster had seemed as much in awe of it as the hens. And the wonder it showed couldn't be fake. Only human beings are capable of that kind of play-acting, or hypocrisy.

"Therefore, the rooster is saying something else when it sings," Basilius concluded. "Before ascribing human emotions and motivations to it the way priests, nationalists and other charlatans have done, I should come back to observe it again tomorrow morning and check to see if it looks at the sun come up with as much wonder every morning."

But to do that he had to stop Levonian from following him. He knew the detective wouldn't rest until he had won. And, exactly the same way he had this morning with his accusations, Levonian would make a scene, he'd miss the rooster's song and his project would be sabotaged.

So, he said to him:

"I was wrong to talk about the blue paradise, even in jest. I'm sorry and I'll do everything I can to make up for it. But not in this novel. No matter what its merits are, if you're the protagonist, it'll be seen as a crime novel and will be forgotten like all the others. However, if you leave me alone, I promise to do what you're asking as soon as I've finished this project."

"And what if between now and then you die of cancer or get dementia?"

"Don't be so pessimistic …"

"How can I not be after everything you've put me through?"

"I'll figure it out and make it work."

"Do it. Now."

"Be reasonable, Vass."

"I was reasonable for thirty years."

"Only two more …"

"No. You get me out of this coma, now, with all the honours that are my due for my many years of service. Otherwise, I'll come back to haunt you night and day. I'll prevent the light of creation from shining on you until the shadows of darkness claim your spirit and your work disappears in the abyss of oblivion and no one ever opens one of your books again and makes me relive the horrors you've put me through."

-23-

BASILIUS KNEW HIS CHARACTER WELL. Levonian never used threats unless he was prepared to act on them. But the policeman didn't come back to plague him that day, or the next when he went back to the henhouse to check to see if the rooster was still looking at the sunrise with as much wonder and was still as surprised each time the sun appeared.

Why? What was the inspector up to now? Basilius wondered as the rooster sang its song in the livid light of dawn and then stood there, still facing the East as though fascinated by the ball of fire rising out of the waves, the hens in a circle around him as dumbstruck as it was.

A moment later, while the sun was growing in strength and its rays were setting the sea on fire, the hens started scratching the ground, cackling and shaking their tails. The rooster stayed there stock still for a moment longer and then, shaking itself as though coming out of its stupor, took a few steps, head held high, and jumped one of the hens and took it from behind.

Basilius pulled out his notebook and wrote: "The rooster sings when it sees the first light of dawn. This is undoubtedly a cry of joy that goes something like: The sun is back! Then, it stays there stock still for a moment not because it doesn't believe its eyes — the rooster knew the light was coming — but to pay homage to the sun which was allowing it to enjoy the pleasures of this world and another day of beauty. To show just how grateful it is, the rooster jumps a hen …"

He didn't have the time to finish his sentence.

Levonian, who had reappeared and was reading his notes over his shoulder, said to him:

"You're off to a bad start, old man."

Basilius slipped his notebook and pen back into his pocket and started walking down the road that led to his house.

"Your judgement is clouded by this theme of yours," Levonian went on as he fell into step beside him. "You so desperately want the rooster's song to be a hymn to life that you're arranging the evidence in such a way as to support your theory, disregarding the golden rule of any investigation: Get rid of all preconceived ideas and only deal with the facts. Only the hard, cold facts should matter. Fact Number One: There is no correlation between the rooster's song and the sun. Roosters sing at night as well as at dawn. You don't hear them because you're asleep. Furthermore, they don't just sing at dawn and at night, they also sing during the day. You must've heard them during the day. But like everyone, you only remember the morning song. Because – Fact Number Two – at that time of day, the rooster is the only bird that sings. We could ask ourselves why that is. Why, of all the animals, only the rooster cries at dawn? And why, of all the songs it sings all day and all night long, it's the one at dawn — Fact Number Three — that's the most powerful? If you want your conclusions to hold water, rather than playing with all sorts of hypotheses, you'll have to deal with these facts, investigate every lead, consider all the possibilities. Otherwise, you're going to be laughed at.

Basilius stopped walking and said:

"OK. Let's stick to the facts then. The rooster is known to sometimes sing at night and in the middle of the afternoon, but more powerfully at dawn."

"Don't forget that at dawn — Fact Number Two — of all the animals in creation, the rooster is the only animal to make its voice heard."

"Maybe the rooster is the only one to have retained, in its genes, the memory of the long night that lead to the death of the dinosaurs? And every morning, at the first light of dawn, it announces to the other beasts that they can eat and procreate for another day."

"Forget your goddam theme for a minute! Fact Number One: Sometimes the rooster sings at night and during the day as well. In which case — for a moment, forget the image you've conjured up of the rooster and follow the opposite reasoning — its song could as easily be a lament. Think of our songs. Human beings have composed thousands and thousands of them. Are they all hymns of joy? I'd say just the opposite. And, we don't wake up in the middle of the night in order to "exult". When we wake up at night, more often than not, it's to lament. You should be asking yourself: what does the rooster have to be sad about?"

Basilius frowned as he gathered his thoughts.

"You've been observing the rooster for two days. Haven't you noticed something that distinguishes it from other animals and more specifically from other feathered animals?"

"It can't be complaining about being surrounded by females all the time and not having other males to shoot the shit with!"

"Look at the notes you took yesterday. You wrote: 'I can't fly, the rooster said to the hens, but I can chase off the darkness and bring you the light.' You've got this idea of the beauty of the world in your head, and because of it you haven't pursued this lead because you're afraid of what it might reveal."

"What lead? What are you talking about?"

"The rooster's wings! Its big beautiful wings. So brilliant and full of colour and of no use whatever. 'I can't fly.'"

"What are you trying to say? That its song is a cry of rage against the laws of gravity?"

"Animals use every member and every organ their creator has given them. Except the rooster. The part of its body which it can't use isn't a lowly claw, but the very essence of its identity: its wings. Human beings don't have wings and they dream of flying. Put yourself in the rooster's place. You're a bird. You've got wings — and beautiful ones at that — but you can't use them. Would you sing with joy when you see your cousins, and cousins a lot less beautiful than you are, flying all day long while you're stuck on the ground? Wouldn't you wake up at night to lament your fate especially if your dreams are full of flight, gliding, diving and soaring? And early in the morning when you see the sun coming up wouldn't you cry out: 'I'm a bird. One of the most majestic! I want to fly, feel the wind under my wings, see the clouds up close, see something vaster and more beautiful than this shitty cage!' Suddenly, the sun comes up over the horizon. Filled with emotion you pray. 'May today be the day that my wings finally live up to their promise!' And then the rooster shakes itself, fluffs its feathers, takes a run for it, lifts off for a few centimeters and plop! ... To drown its sorrow, it jumps a hen ..."

Basilius smiles.

"Hey, the golden rule, think maybe you've forgotten it too?"

WHEN MURIEL GOT OUT of bed that day, her husband, his brow furrowed, was already settled at his work table looking at his notes.

"I got up earlier this morning to have a pee and you weren't on the terrace …"

"I went for a walk."

"Yesterday too, when I got up …"

"I went for a walk."

"At dawn …"

"Yes, at dawn," Basilius answered as he looked down at his notes again.

Muriel watched him for a moment.

"Making headway?"

"Yes."

She left without asking another question. She washed, dressed and then left the house to do some shopping, see some friends and let her husband work in peace.

When she got back for lunch around one o'clock, Basilius was still sitting at his writing table asking himself if the rooster's song was a song of joy the way he'd imagined it, or a cry of rage the way Levonian maintained.

He was well aware that his policeman had suggested this to confuse him, instil doubt and sabotage his project. All the same, because he was a rational man, he couldn't dismiss the possibility that the rooster's song was the lament of a bird incapable of flying.

"Before deciding, I should visit a few more henhouses and observe how other roosters behave at sunrise," he said to himself just as Muriel returned from her walk and asked if he had heard from their daughter.

"No."

Muriel prepared a light meal and, as she was eating, she told her husband that Alicia was hosting a supper that evening and they were invited.

"Would it bother you to go alone?" Basilius answered. "I have to go to bed early. I've got to be up before dawn."

"Why? Do you have a date with a chick?"

Surprised, Basilius looked up at her.

"Nicolas Laïos saw you, staked out in front of a henhouse two mornings in a row. He maintains that he heard you talking to the chickens. And he tells anyone who'll listen that because you've written so much about murder and killers, something's gone screwy in your head, because otherwise you'd be interested in his story. It doesn't take much to fuel island gossip, Leo. So little happens here that they blow up the tiniest little tidbit, embellishing it and turning it into a soap-opera. Normally I wouldn't give it a second thought, but I've seen you staring at henhouses during our walks …"

She took her husband's hand.

"Why are you so interested in chickens, Leo? This morning you told me your work has started up again. Can I ask? Are chickens part of your new writing project? Is that why you have to get up before dawn tomorrow morning?"

"Stop talking to me with that tone of voice."

"What tone of voice?"

"The tone people use when they want to spare the feelings of a madman."

"Alright, then answer me. What's your new project about?"

"I don't know yet!"

There was such frustration and such anguish in his answer that tears sprang to Muriel's eyes.

"Why don't you write a crime novel, my love?"

"Let's not start that again! I explained it all to you!"

"That's true. You did explain everything to me. Except it doesn't seem to be working. I can see that and it breaks my heart. What's the idea of changing genres at your age? We shouldn't change anything at our age, my love. It can only do harm."

"Stop, Muriel."

"Luckily, you didn't kill Levonian …"

"Stop!"

"I can't stop! Put yourself in my place, damn it! You don't laugh anymore. And you don't talk. You don't want to have anything to do with our daughter's separation. You don't show me affection of any kind anymore. And when you decide to go to bed with me, ten minutes afterwards I hear you muttering the name Loraine in your sleep. And what do I discover this morning? Loraine could be the name of a chicken. A real chicken that lays eggs. Return to the crime novel, my love. The age of metamorphoses is over. The gods in this country no longer change themselves into swans and young girls into spiders. Return to the crime novel, call Clara to find out how she's doing and come to supper with me tonight at Alicia's and show them all that you're not crazy. Alicia even prepared some little vegetarian dishes just for you."

Basilius pushed back his chair, got up from his worktable and left the house.

-25-

T HE SUN WAS SCORCHING HOT and cicadas by the thousands filled the air with their cries. In his rush to leave the house, he'd forgotten his sunglasses and hat and the light from the sky and its glare off the earth hit him in the eyes and made sweat run down his forehead, temples, chest and back, completely soaking his shirt. But he didn't move into the shade or slow his pace. Levonian was hard on his heels like a snarling dog. He was afraid that if he stopped, he'd end up answering him and people would see him talking to himself again.

"Why didn't you tell her about the rooster?" the policeman asked. "If you're so proud of your discovery, why didn't you say something? You took three wives from me. Are you afraid of what yours will think of your idea?"

Without turning around, Basilius raised two fingers.

"Three!" Levonian countered. "You don't even remember! You rubbed out three not two! In the first novel, I was a young married man. But the only times I talked to my wife was on the phone when I'd call to tell her I'd be home late because I was investigating the bastards who'd sent a native kid to jail for a crime he didn't commit. I didn't have a single meal with her. I never held her in my arms. Not even once. Even if moments like those must've made up a good half of my existence. No wonder she ended up cheating on me and leaving …

"To drown my sorrow, I spent all my free time drinking. Only the bottle smiled at me. Until five books later, I met a woman whose smile warmed my heart and lit up my days. And she was a fellow cop who understood my work and its demands. She never made me feel bad about the long hours I had to put in. I told myself that at last I'd found my soul mate, the woman I could spend the rest of my life with. And you let me kid myself and love her more than I'd ever loved anyone before. And so, my grief was even greater when I lost her. Gill had barely begun to heal my battered heart when you shot her in the head with a bullet intended for me.

"Same thing with Véronique. Have you forgotten her too? I still mourn her. Still cry. Because when I lost her, I also lost the child she was carrying.

"My first child.

"I was so moved when she told me that she was pregnant — flying high, jubilant.

"You can't have forgotten that too! It was in the first chapter of the twelfth book. The only book where you had me leave town. You'd decided to set the novel in the idyllic spot where you spent summers with your family. I'd just arrived at the cottage I'd rented, when I ran into a gang of druggies who, after knocking me out, raped and killed the love of my life and the only child I might have had.

"Why, Leo? To exorcise the anxiety you felt in those northern woods? Or was it because you really wanted your own wife out of the picture and, since you didn't have the courage to dump her, the women who loved me and whom I loved paid the price?"

Basilius was wandering around aimlessly and only stopped when he found himself at the edge of a cliff. The same one with the remains of the temple dedicated to Dionysos where, at twenty-two, he and Loraine would watch the sun set. There wasn't even the hint of a breeze here either even though it was exposed to the four winds.

"You gave my fellow cops spouses and families," Levonian went on, oblivious to the wild beauty of the place and the melancholy created by the fragments of Ionic columns that the centuries had transformed into the gravestones of a once great civilization.

"In novel after novel, they'd show me pictures of their children as they grew up and tell me what they said when they were two, four, or ten years old. Why couldn't I have had the same pictures to show around, the same stories to tell? Because the *perfect sleuth* has to be a solitary man, a stoic to the core with nothing to distract him from his investigations and get in the way of the novel's dramatic build. Then, why even bring Naomi, Gill and Véronique into my life? To present a new side of me to the reader? To show them that if, at work, I keep my distance and don't allow myself to be overcome with emotion, in my private life, I can be as sensitive and tender as the next guy? But did Gill and Véronique have to pay with their lives in order to pull that off?

"When your daughter was hit by a car when she was four, you spent two weeks by her bedside at the hospital because your wife had to take care of your newborn son. Maybe you've forgotten this too? When the call came through about the accident, you were in the middle of getting me to light a cigarette. Do you have any idea what it's like for a smoker to wait two weeks to light up? I'd have donated one of my kidneys to science if I could've had even a couple of drags. But I understood. You were worried. And it was only a car accident. You killed my baby and the woman who was carrying it and you didn't even give me time to mourn them. Because nothing was supposed to slow down my pursuit of their killers.

"Even my friends … You made me insanely loyal in my friendships which you then ruined, one by one, by getting my friends to betray me …

"Why all these deaths and betrayals, Leo? All the lost lights, all the sorrow? The women I loved. The child I was waiting for. The friends and colleagues I lost. Did they live and die only as dramatic triggers to spice up your stories and make you rich and famous? If at least you could remember their names and the families who mourned them and who will continue to mourn them every time a reader opens one of your books and reads the lines you wrote about them …

"But no one will shed a tear for me.

"Novel after novel, you sent me knocking on the doors of people who were calmly living their lives, to announce the death of a child, a sister, a husband. It's a lousy job. One you never get used to. Nevertheless, I did it. I'd find the words and empathize with them in their grief. Total strangers. As for me, your most faithful companion, you take advantage of my loyalty for thirty years, then you close the circle of my life by putting me in a coma without even announcing my passing!

"Why? To keep a door open in case you can't pull off your masterpiece? Why not at least let the readers mourn me? Were you afraid the announcement of my death would affect the sales of the other sixteen novels? And if that's the case, you're not only the biggest serial killer I know, but you're also the most despicable of hypocrites. And I can't denounce you or beat you up. All I can do is damn you and haunt you. But no matter how powerful you are, the only way you can stifle my voice is by making me your rooster. A rooster who will finally fly far away from this shitty awful mess you've put me in."

"Let him talk," Basilius said to himself. "He's hurt. And with good reason. So, let him blow off some steam. Concentrate on the song of the rooster. That's what'll shut him up once and for all. All I have to do is decide if the rooster's song is one of joy or of rage."

-26-

H E GOT BACK HOME as night was falling.
Muriel was waiting for him, sitting in front of an empty bottle of wine holding a full glass, her eyes hazy, her tongue thick and coated.

"So, is your plan for immortality moving forward nicely?"

He went into the kitchen and poured himself a glass of water.

"I looked for you everywhere," his wife said following him. "Do you have any idea how worried I was?"

"I'm back. In one piece. Stop yelling."

"I have every reason to yell, don't you think? Here I am stranded at the other end of the world with a husband who's running after chickens. At least, during your first stay here, you talked to the sirens," she added, referring to one of his short stories inspired by Nysa in which a young hippie high on pot thinking he's seen a siren, throws himself into the sea and begs her to stop and talk to him.

"Let's go home, Leo. Please. You're too old to be tempting the devil. Let's pack our bags and go home."

He wanted to answer that he wasn't ready to leave, but the telephone started ringing.

"Go answer," Muriel said. "It's probably one of your children."

"How do you know?"

"I called them. I had to talk to somebody. If I'd called someone on the island, they'd have come for you with a straitjacket. Answer the phone."

"I have nothing to say."

"But they want to talk to you."

"To say what? Tell me how to succeed as a couple, from a daughter who's changed partners four times in the last ten years? Or maybe what I should write about, from two sons who have trouble reading a book all the way to the end?"

"You're turning your back on your children now too?"

"Go to bed, Muriel, you're drunk."

He poured himself another glass of water, then opened the fridge to put the water bottle back and find something to eat.

When he turned around, Muriel was no longer in the kitchen. The phone had stopped ringing and, thinking she'd gone to answer it, he took the plate of food he'd prepared and went out on the terrace to eat.

In the soft light that precedes the rising of the moon, Muriel was heading down to the sea, taking her clothes off as she went and scattering them on the ground behind her.

A little further off, some teenagers were filming her on their phones and laughing.

Basilius left the terrace and ran after her. But when he got to the shore, his wife had already thrown herself into the sea stark naked.

She was so drunk she could drown, so he jumped in the water all dressed and reached her in a few strokes.

"We never swam in the nude," she said to him. "I know I'm no siren, not even close, but in the dark …"

She clung to him.

"I saw you ogling her, you know. She noticed it too. Why do you think she prepared those vegetarian dishes for you? But there'll always be a place for your slippers under my bed. Thirty-five years, isn't nothing …"

He didn't say anything even if he was annoyed with her. Especially for introducing him to Nicholas Laïos. If, to spite him, the old Greek hadn't told the whole island he'd seen him talking to himself outside a henhouse, they wouldn't be there floating around like two survivors of a shipwreck. Still, he said nothing. In her present state, his wife wouldn't have heard or remembered a thing anyway. He just nodded his head while he got her out of the water, took her back up to the house, dried her off and put her to bed.

Two minutes later, she was snoring.

BASILIUS PUT ON SOME DRY CLOTHES and went and sat on the terrace in the dark. He didn't touch the plate of food he'd prepared for himself. Alcohol would've gone down better but he had to keep his mind clear so he could think about the events of the day and how he was going to extricate himself from them.

"Go home to Canada," Levonian suggested.

"I could've done without him right now!" he thought. "But I can't hold his perseverance against him. That's how I made him. To be a fighter and never give up. Might as well resign myself to his presence and his comments."

"You haven't succeeded in making your sons read a novel all the way to the end," said the policeman, "and yet you want people to believe that their salvation depends on the ability of a bird who can't fly to be happy? Forget the goddam rooster, Leo. Delete it from your thoughts and take your wife back to Canada before she drowns for real."

Basilius closed his eyes in an attempt to think.

"If I had had children and grand-children," Levonian continued, back on Basilius' case as though he was a suspect he was grilling, "I would've even given up the blue paradise to stay close to them."

"He never misses a chance to bring up his damn paradise," thought Basilius.

"Animals prepare themselves all their lives for one moment. You said as much in the twelfth novel when you talked about how hormones rule our lives. There is only one reason for the existence of males and females — procreation. Why not me? The joys of continuity which my children provided would've been enough to give meaning to all my hard work and to time passing by. Watching them grow, I could've seen, through them, the child I'd once been. Because you didn't give me a childhood either. Not a single memory of my parents. Not a photo. Who were they? What did they look like? What did they do? Nothing. It was as if I didn't exist beyond the murders, the crimes and the filthy, disgusting things people do to each other."

"The copper sure has a lot to get off his chest!" thought Basilius, without letting anything show, convinced that Levonian was only going on like this to soften him up so he'd pull him out of the coma.

"Think about it. In the thousands of pages you devoted to my police investigations, there may be no more than a dozen references to my adolescence. The lyrics to an old hit parade tune I still knew by heart. A book or a film which meant a lot to me when I was young. But nothing about my childhood. Nothing about my parents. If we were to transcribe the interviews you've given in the course of the past thirty years, there'd be two hundred pages minimum where you talk about your family history and background. The dog you had when you were a kid probably gets a dozen. Shit, even the murderers in your novels got a one, or two, page bio. And that's not counting the chapters in which I dug into their pasts as well as the pasts of their victims. And yet, I knew practically nothing about my own past.

"Sure, people are more interested in the bad guy than the cop who's chasing after him. Still, to have no memory of a mother's touch, the look in a father's eyes, the first time you kissed a girl … I'm more than just a policeman married to death, dammit. What are my origins? Where do I come from? Why is my name Levonian and not something else? What did I look like when I was five years old? What did I dream about when I was ten? You must know. We spent sixteen novels together. You must've given some thought to my childhood, right?"

Basilius was thinking of Muriel. The best thing to do was to talk to her about the rooster. His wife had always felt excluded from his writing life. Well, he'd take her with him to the henhouse. Luckily, he'd spotted a few others during his long walkabout that day. Muriel might even notice things he hadn't.

"I'm not in the habit of playing the victim and bemoaning my fate," Levonian said. "I want to know, that's all. You made me like this. If I can't ask you these questions, who can I ask?"

His voice had lost its assurance. To pull himself together, he took out his pack of cigarettes and his lighter.

"For sixteen novels, you've been in command and I've obeyed. Is it too much to want to retire to a blue paradise, with a few childhood memories, a photo of my parents, and a wife who'll give me a child or two?"

Basilius stood up, picked up his plate and went into the house, saying to himself: "I'll bring my camera. If people are spying on me, what I'm doing will look more serious with Muriel and a camera. And I could film the rooster, and then look at it and listen to it as much as I want in my office."

-28-

THE NEXT MORNING, when Basilius wanted to talk to his wife about his project, she said:

"Too late."

She'd thought a lot during the night. And rather than spend three more months chatting and drinking at friends' houses on the island and getting in her husband's way, she'd decided to go home, take care of their daughter and start her volunteer work again.

"Relax," she added when she saw Basilius stiffen. "I'm not going to ask you to come back with me. That's the last thing I need — you accusing me of preventing you from realizing your dream. You can come home when you've written what you came to Nysa to write. All I ask is could you call the airline to change the date of my return flight and take care of the cat."

He called the airline and then even accompanied his wife as she did the rounds, seeing people she wanted to say goodbye to.

The Hungerford sisters, sitting together next to a fan decorated with ribbons — pink for one, blue for the other — were sad to see Muriel leave, but delighted to find out that her husband was staying. They even let him hold the small statue Muriel had told him about so that, when he wrote his novel, he could better describe what they had felt the day they found it.

At the painter's, Alicia said to Muriel:

"It's too bad you're leaving now. The tenor smashed his dentures so he wouldn't be able to eat anymore. It'll be interesting to see if his better half feeds him with a baby bottle or lets him die of hunger."

"Let Leo know what happens and he can write to me about it," Muriel answered.

The next day, accompanied by her husband, she took the boat for Athens.

At the airport, before boarding, she gave him a sealed envelope.

"I asked Sean to do your astrological birth chart. I know you don't believe in astrology but if it can make you laugh and bring back your good humour, that'll be a plus."

She gave him a big hug.

"I also asked Alicia to bring you a few of her vegetarian dishes when she makes some," she added and then left.

There was only one boat for Nysa each day and it left in the morning. So Basilius spent the rest of that day and night in Athens.

Was it the fact that he found himself in a big city? A big city as busy and noisy as Athens where the sunrise was greeted with the honking of a thousand car horns and the lapping of the waves replaced by the frenetic movement of traffic. His obsession with the song of the rooster seemed so insane to him now. It reminded him of his father when he came down with Alzheimer's. One night, at dinner, when he realized, in a moment of lucidity, the absurdity of his preoccupations, he grabbed the carving knife and said to his son: "If I wanted to plunge this into my heart, would you say I'd gone mad? Would you stop me?" Basilius had been so taken aback by the question that he was speechless for a moment. By the end of that moment, the old man had already forgotten why he was holding the knife in his hand.

In the hotel bar, where he drank two glasses of scotch before going upstairs to bed, he asked the barman if he knew what roosters were saying when they crowed. It was a matter of checking whether his idea was as silly as he imagined it to be.

The barman thought for a moment and then said:

"Coffee! I want my coffee!"

Basilius burst out laughing. It was hardly the answer he was looking for, but it was funny. Better yet, rather than look at him as though he was a raving idiot or answer with something commonplace like roosters sing to announce the dawn, the man had taken the time to actually think about the question.

This put him in a better mood and reminded him of the envelope Muriel had given him. He opened it and took out two single-spaced, typewritten pages.

The chart contained all the usual astrological calculations, a description of the character traits of a Sagittarius, his astrological sign, as well as predictions and recommendations which could apply to half of humanity. However, he read the last paragraph three times.

"You are at a turning point in your career which could lead you to heights you have not explored so far. However, it's not easy to enter new paths when you're a Sagittarius with Leo rising: your tendency is to refer to the past and compare what has been with what is and with what could be. Forget all that. Dive into the unknown and recognize that you have created limitations for yourself which do not exist. Our greatest regrets are the risks we didn't take."

He pondered these lines for the rest of the evening.

What is man most afraid of?

Who said that?

What is man most afraid of?

That was the question.

And the answer, perhaps not in these exact terms, was:

A new way, a new idea, even a new word uttered.

"Could that be what's happening to me?" he asked himself. "My new project inspires me and terrifies me at the same time? I want to free myself from the crime-investigation-solution formula with all its conventions. I want to take risks and try something new. But I'm afraid of the unknown. And so, I've invented an alibi, an out — Levonian and his grievances. As shrewd as he is, he figured this out and is taking advantage of my reluctance and using it for his own purposes."

"Dostoevsky," he said suddenly. "That's who said it. Dostoevsky."

That the quote about man's greatest fear came from Dostoevsky gave Sean Costello's advice even more authority and Basilius said to himself: "If you want to make the most of the peace and quiet Muriel has just offered you, stop going back and forth on this and decide: song of joy or song of rage?"

The meltemi, the strong Etesian winds out of the north that bring fresh air to the Aegean in the summer and which everyone had been waiting for eagerly all through July and August — two months during which the highest temperatures in a century had been recorded — started blowing the next day during the crossing and there were whitecaps as far as the eye could see. This was something Basilius couldn't help but interpret as a good omen.

-29-

As soon as he got back to Nysa, Basilius made himself a coffee and re-read his notes.

An hour later, he added a conclusion:

"Until now, all you've done is reason. You have to stop. In order to decipher the rooster's song, to know whether it's a song of joy or of rage, you'll have to think of the rooster in rooster terms, put yourself in its skin, live what it's living, feel its wings, get a sense of its feathers, its companions, the ground it scratches, the henhouse, absorb its essence, fill your lungs, your heart and your mind with it, until it becomes part of you and you become a rooster."

"Now you've gone completely bonkers," Levonian said. He was leaning over his creator's shoulder again to see what he was writing.

Basilius didn't even look at him. The next day, at dawn, he set himself up with his camera in front of a hen house, eyes wide open, ears alert, nostrils dilated, ready to capture with his body, his flesh, everything about the way the rooster moved, scratched for food, or shat.

"You're wasting your time," Levonian said. "You have about as much of a chance of getting into its skin as you do of laying an egg."

Basilius ignored him, the same way he ignored the pass-ers-by who stopped to look at him. He only left when the sun, at its peak, scorched the island with its rays, forcing even the chickens to take refuge in the henhouse in search of some shade.

· Back home, his cop still in tow, Basilius transferred the pictures he'd taken to his laptop so he could look at them on a larger screen.

"I'm so impressed. Wow! An artist in the act of creating!" the detective teased.

Basilius put on his headphones, plugged them into his computer and turned the volume up to maximum.

Levonian was so angry at not being heard anymore he was almost apoplectic. Meanwhile Basilius, his eyes glued to the screen, was saying: "Help me, rooster. When you sense the sun is about to rise, are you cursing it with your song or are you singing a hymn to life?"

For two whole days, locked behind closed doors at home, shutters drawn, he played the images and sounds he'd captured at the henhouse over and over again, trying to guess the meaning of the song that erupted from the rooster's body every morning, without finding an answer to the question that obsessed him.

For the novel he wanted to write, he hoped that these images would, beyond a shadow of a doubt, support his the-ory that the rooster called to the sun each night and at dawn it sang the glory of the day that was breaking. But as soon as one detail supported this theory, another came along to con-tradict it. And vice-versa. No sooner had he concluded that the rooster was fed up with its fate than an image would appear to show the rooster wasn't the least bit distressed.

If Levonian couldn't tear his headphones off his head, the cat didn't hesitate to rub up against his legs when it was hungry. But the fridge was empty. There was no food for the cat or for him and, since his eyes and his thoughts had started to lose focus, he decided to go out, buy some food and have a beer at the café to take his mind off things.

"Cock-a-doodle-doo!" he heard some children yell as soon as he put his nose out the door.

At first, he didn't pay any attention, thinking the children were just playing. But when he walked into the grocery store, he sensed that people were watching him, elbowing each other and whispering behind his back. When he finally arrived at the café, he saw the waiter say something to two customers and wink in his direction. This time, he got the distinct impression that the three men were laughing at him.

Basilius stood there for a moment wondering whether he should just ignore them or go home, pack his bags and leave for another island where he could rent a house with its own henhouse and observe the rooster as much as he wanted without being disturbed.

That's what he was thinking when Alicia arrived looking fresh and smiling.

She'd stopped by the house yesterday, she said, had even phoned him, but he hadn't answered. Either the door or the telephone.

"I even went around and checked at a few henhouses …"

She seemed to be in the know as well.

"D'you think I'm completely off my rocker?"

"I'm sure you have a perfectly good reason to be observing the chickens."

He never talked about a novel while he was writing it. But he was so encouraged by her words and the attention she was lavishing on him that he said:

"It's not the hens I'm interested in. I'm trying to understand what the rooster is saying every morning when it sings."

"That's so interesting!" Alicia exclaimed. "I never imagined it could be saying anything other than announcing the sun rise."

Basilius was so delighted by her reaction that he invited her to have a beer with him so he could talk to her a little more about his project, but Alicia was in a hurry. A friend was waiting for her.

"Come meet me tomorrow at the little creek where I swim every morning after my run. We'll be alone just the two of us. At last. And we can talk without being interrupted or stared at."

He no longer noticed the amused looks people exchanged or the elbow-jabs as he walked by, didn't even hear the children's cock-a-doodle-doos. As he set out on the road home with his bag of groceries, all he could see was Alicia's smiling face and hear her voice so full of promises.

"That's so interesting!"

And then:

"We'll be alone just the two of us. At last ..."

She had even come to his house and knocked on his door. Had phoned him. But with his headphones on, he hadn't heard a thing.

-30-

He woke three times that night convinced each time that the sun had come up. The fourth time, he got out of bed, shaved, took a shower and got dressed. He looked in the mirror trying to find his least grandfatherly profile.

"You're going to look really appealing in the nude with your sixty-something genitals on full display," Levonian said to him. "If you want to get laid, find a woman your own age who won't laugh when after she's barely begun to work on your pecker, your new-found exuberance slips away like an old man's fart."

"Meow," said the cat rubbing up against Basilius' legs: "Don't let that bastard bring you down with his negativity. It's Alicia who put you on the trail of the rooster in the cemetery and because of that he's afraid she'll also help you solve the mystery of its song. That's why Muriel told you to take care of me, so I can remind you that only the beautiful cook of those little vegetarian dishes can lead you to the new heights her uncle, the astrologist, predicted for you."

Basilius fed the cat, had a piece of toast and a coffee and then, with his beach towel under his arm, he set out for the creek where Alicia was waiting for him.

Pure chance? Or another sign? It was the same creek as the one where he used to swim with Loraine, the young

American, who according to Muriel had inspired his best short story.

Oh, the ingenuousness of youth! Back then, he didn't worry about the figure he cut or about his erectile functioning any more than he did about cancer or Alzheimer's. There were ten times more henhouses on the island in those days and a rooster sang outside his window every morning. But its cock-a-doodle-doos, like the chirping of the cicada which accompanied his first steps as a writer the rest of the day, all said the same thing — he knew this beyond a shadow of a doubt — life, life, life!

Would Alicia succeed in convincing him that nothing had changed?

The cicadas were already singing all around him. The meltemi was blowing heavy with the soft smells of pine, sage and sea spray. On the water, gentle ripples ran from the rising sun to the shore.

But, no one was waiting for him at the creek.

"Good lord!" said Levonian. "Did our beautiful muse stand us up?"

Basilius sat in the shade of an outcropping and looked at the tiny waves breaking on the beach. He was wondering if once again he'd let himself be taken in when, suddenly, the voice he had so hoped to hear rang out:

"Here I am! I'm coming!"

The cicadas got louder while Basilius' heart started racing.

"I'm coming!" she shouted again as she raced down the slope, a whirlwind full of life and enthusiasm.

"You're here!" she said, out of breath, when at last she came to a stop in front of him. "Thank you, thank you!" she added taking off her helmet, untying and shaking out her long hair.

She was wearing a small back pack which she removed and opened taking out a towel and a bottle of water. She wiped away the sweat that was dripping into her eyes and took a long drink of water. He drank her in with his eyes.

"Do you want some?"

"No, thank you."

She put the top back on the bottle and set it down in the shade.

"How many kilometres do you run every morning?"

He'd come here to seduce her but couldn't stop himself from being nice — a kind of paternal niceness.

"Ten."

She described her route to him as she took off her running shoes, socks and, as if it was the most natural thing in the world, her t-shirt, shorts and panties.

"You're not getting undressed?"

The chirping of the cicadas echoed in his head.

"Later ..."

"I'm covered in sweat. I've got to go in."

She turned around and headed for the water.

"What a man! A real satyr," Levonian teased. "Even the cicadas are laughing their heads off!"

He was ready to let rip with a few more insults, but Alicia had turned around and was walking back towards him.

"I have a small favour to ask of you."

She crouched down in front of him and, during what seemed like an eternity, she went digging in her bag.

"I talked to Muriel about this. She told me not to bother you with it, that you were very busy."

She took what looked like a five-hundred-page manuscript out of her back pack.

"I've been working on it for four years. I thought Drew would help me with it but you know what he's like and what he thinks of detective novels. Even when I make changes, he still thinks it's shit. To be frank, I'm convinced he's jealous and I'm seriously thinking of breaking up with him."

She handed him the manuscript.

"D'you think you could take a quick look while I go for a swim? I'd really like to know what you think. It's my first novel. I'm sure it needs work, but I'm ready to start over. Line by line, if I have to.

She had stood up and her pubic hair was level with Basilius' eyes.

"That is, of course, if you have time. I wouldn't want to impose."

She turned her back on him again and ran down towards the water. Levonian's tone had changed as he said:

"Only the crime novel, Leo, only the crime novel paints a true portrait of humanity. The little bitch! Not a single word about the rooster's song! And she won't just be satisfied with your notes. Oh no! She'll sweet talk you, cajole you and take up all your time until you've recommended her manuscript to your publisher or your agent as well as written a quote for the back cover praising her work. But he who laughs last, laughs best, eh. Bring me here for a few days to recover from my injuries and I'll teach the little cock teaser some manners!"

Basilius shook his head.

"It's harder and harder these days for someone who's not known to even get their manuscript read. Anyway, why did

I come here to meet her? To talk to her about my writing. My problems, my worries. She just beat me to it, that's all."

"Don't tell me you're going to help her!"

Basilius shook his head again.

"No time. She's got her whole life ahead of her. I don't."

He took out his pen and wrote on the manuscript: "I can't right now. Sorry." And left it there on the beach.

Offshore, Alicia was raising and falling with the waves floating like a mirage. And as he walked back up the hill, the air around him heavy with the chirping of cicadas, he thought of the young hippie in one of his stories who, high on pot and thinking he'd seen a siren, threw himself in the water so he could catch up with her.

31

A WEEK LATER, Alicia received a phone call from Muriel asking her whether she had news of her husband.

"I haven't seen him since you left," the young woman answered.

"Not even on the terrace, mornings, when you jog?"

"I've changed routes."

"Why?"

"Why not? Why all these questions?"

Because her husband hadn't been in touch, Muriel answered. She kept calling him and sending him emails, but hadn't received an answer. She was worried.

"Could you go check and see if he's okay and tell him to call me?"

Alicia promised her that she'd talk to Basilius, but instead asked her uncle to go tell the writer to call his wife.

"He'll jump my bones. His wife had barely left the island, before he came to find me at the creek. He kept staring at me and tried hustling me. I couldn't tell his wife that. And I can't send Drew. He's so jealous, especially of other people's success, he'd probably bash his teeth in."

Sean Costello went to Basilius's house. He didn't mention the incident at the creek even though he wished Basilius would go back and try again, if only for the pleasure of seeing Drew cuckolded.

As he would say later, the astrologist found the writer less chatty than usual, a little more morose and distracted, but that didn't surprise him coming from a man in the throes of creation. When Farley was struggling with his chairs, how often had he locked himself inside his studio for days on end, so lost in his artistic explorations that he forgot the world and that included his lover. Plus, the meltemi had been blowing non-stop for ten days with enough force and tenacity to unhinge people as well as awnings. There was no doubt about it, those dreadful Etesian winds could put anyone on edge, especially if you were living in a house right on the sea where they blow the strongest.

"Even his own wife didn't notice anything unusual when Basilius called her after my visit like I'd asked him to," Costello said. "Okay, he forgot to ask about their daughter. Again. But Muriel was delighted with their conversation, especially seeing as how her husband told her he only had one small problem to solve before he'd be able to free himself of the shackles of the crime novel and reach the heights I'd predicted for him. Even the Hungerford twins, who had done as much research on ageing as they had on the famous Battle of Nysa, hadn't noticed anything when they ran into him a few days after my visit."

The meltemi had finally blown itself out. Not a leaf was stirring in the trees on September 8, at dawn, the anniversary of the death of Corporal Hungerford.

The way they did every year on that day, the twins, both dressed in black, were heading for the bay where the British brigades had landed to liberate the island from the Germans and, at exactly 6:30, to meditate, at the spot where their father had lost his life and go through the commemorative rituals they observed on every anniversary of his death.

The whole island was asleep with the exception of Leo Basilius. Sitting in front of a henhouse, he seemed totally lost in contemplation of its occupants. He was, in fact, startled when the two women said hello and invited him to go to the Bay of Pounta with them.

The astrologist finished his story:

"The Hungerford sisters can say, now, that he should have shown less interest in the chickens and more in the sacrifice their father had made because there was nothing like the carnages of war to bring a person firmly back down to earth. However, three hours later, when they made their way back from the Bay of Pounta, they didn't ask themselves why Basilius was still there in front of the henhouse because there was nothing — and I repeat — nothing to indicate that, if he was still there, it was because he couldn't remember how to get back home."

32

He wasn't alone. But that was something the two sisters couldn't see.

He was with Levonian, who was saying:

"The rooster, the rooster. You see where it gets you to keep chewing on the same old bone?"

"And what about your Paradise, eh?" Basilius shot back. His tone was so violent that the chickens, frightened, moved off with a chorus of cackling. "I'd be in front of my keyboard, my fingers and my grey matter working at full speed, if you hadn't plagued me with your damn paradise! So, get off my back!"

Levonian's tone changed as well.

"OK, I won't say another word. Calm down. You've gotta stay calm. Otherwise, we'll never get out of here."

For a moment, neither said a word. Worried, Levonian watched his creator look right and then left, again and again, and then sigh:

"Poor Leo, are you already tittering on the edge of the abyss? Come on, don't give up. You've repeated that to me often enough."

"Two directions, Vass. Only two and I can't seem to decide."

"You've forgotten that's all. No big deal. Happens to everyone in periods of stress no matter what their age. All you have to do is stay calm. You've gotten us out of tougher situations than this. Stay calm and you'll get us out this time too."

"Yes, I've got to, I've got to …"

Again, Basilius looked right and then left, and right again, left, until tears filled his eyes.

"Leo …

The policeman wanted to take him in his arms, console him, shake him too to put some life back into him, but of course he couldn't touch him.

So, he said:

"Listen to me carefully. You listening?"

"Yes."

"You're all-powerful. D'you hear what I'm saying?"

"Yes."

"You are the all-powerful creator of thousands of wonders and thousands of horrors. The man who, with a single word, builds a world, gives life and takes it away, makes the rain pour down and the snow fall to the earth, dries the oceans and makes the fields bloom. Nothing is impossible for you. You destroy the vile plans of the bad guys, avenge the innocent, punish the guilty, give hope to the weak and heal broken hearts. Do you understand what I'm saying?"

"Nothing is impossible for me."

"Exactly, my friend. Now, look at the henhouse."

"We're supposed to be looking for the direction of …"

"Look at the henhouse, goddam it."

"Alright, I'm looking."

"The front."

"Yes."

"What's it facing?"

"The sea."

"What's at the other end of the sea?"

"… Nothing."

"Think. At the end of the sea, there's … the hori …? The hori …? The horizon!"

"Of course. So?"

"Ah, nothing harder to pin down than the obvious."

"What are you talking about?"

"The horizon, Leo. And not just any horizon either. The front of the henhouse is facing the horizon where the sun comes up every morning. Why, do you think?"

"…"

"Try …"

"Okay. Yes, I'm thinking."

"The front of a henhouse always faces east."

"We don't know if every henhouse …

"I checked."

"Ah? Why didn't you tell me?"

"I forgot."

"Oh, yeah?"

"Happens to everyone."

"Huh-huh."

"Anyway, the front of a henhouse always faces east. And if you'd observed the other feathered creatures as much as you did the rooster, you would've noticed that they all like to sleep facing east. Could it be because they want to wake with the first rays of daylight and not miss a moment of life?"

"Hmmm. If the rooster is so keen to live …"

"Its song can only be a song of joy. That's why, as soon as it sees the sun, it mounts a chicken. Would you make children, if you thought life was the shits?"

"And the rooster's frustration and rage at not being able to fly?"

"Leo, novel after novel, even when every illusion I harboured proved to be a bitter one, I kept at it and kept dreaming of my little paradise. Even now in a coma, every fibre of my body dreams of a glorious resurrection in a place where the ocean will erase all the wrinkles in my heart and all my wishes will come true. Because that's the way you made me. And you made me this way because every creator programmes his creations to hope no matter what. Even when faced with the inevitable. The same for the rooster. He is so full of hope that all obstacles become mirages. And every dawn, it sees in the rising sun the promise of a new day of flights and odysseys."

A smile lit up Basilius' face.

"I owe you one, Vass."

"Make me your rooster's friend."

"Yes. There's got to be a way to do that. But first I have to find the word that'll best render its cock-a-doodle-doo."

"You'll find it."

"I'll find it, yes, I'll find it. As soon as we get home."

Again, he looked to the right and then to the left.

"Help me, Vass. Otherwise Loraine will be worried and she won't let me leave the house anymore."

About the Author

PAN BOUYOUCAS is a prize-winning Montreal novelist, playwright and translator whose novels and plays have been translated into several languages. Two of his novels were written originally in English: *The Man Who Wanted to Drink Up the Sea*, which was selected by France's FNAC as one of the 12 best novels of 2005, and *The Tattoo*, which was longlisted for the 2012 Re-Lit Award. *Cock-A-Doodle-Doo* is the third of Pan's French-language novels to be translated into English under the Guernica imprint, the previous two being *A Father's Revenge* (2001) and *Portrait of a Husband with the Ashes of His Wife (2018)*.

About the Translator

MAUREEN LABONTÉ is a translator, dramaturge and teacher. She has coordinated a number of play development programmes in theatres and play development centres across the country. Maureen has also worked extensively as a translation dramaturge. Since 2012, she has been the coordinator of the Playwrights Workshop Montreal/Cole Foundation Mentorship for Emerging Translators. This highly successful programme is now in its seventh cycle. She has translated close to fifty plays into English. *And Slowly Beauty*, her translation of *Lentement la beauté*, by Michel Nadeau, published by Talonbooks, was shortlisted for the 2014 Governor General's Award in Translation. She lives in Montreal.

MIX
Paper
FSC® C100212
www.fsc.org

Printed in January 2022
by Gauvin Press,
Gatineau, Québec